猴塞雷

雅思聽力7+

You don't have to be a one trick pony

首度公開**4**大突破重點，如何有效突破?!

由聽力關鍵字彙+聽力題型+口譯技巧+模擬試題

➡ **雅思聽力高分**

武董◎著

專業英籍老師錄製MP3

突破重點1：掌握聽力關鍵字彙
量身打造聽力字彙單元，精選聽力考試中生活場景與學術場景常考字彙

突破重點2：熟悉聽力題型
詳盡分析雅思聽力七大題型，迅速掌握解題要領

突破重點3：口譯的Shadowing(跟讀)**和Recall**(回想)**提升聽力理解力與專注力**
聽力理解力(Listening Comprehension)與專注力(Concentration)遠比記筆記、考試技巧和機經重要

突破重點4：兩回模擬試題強化應考實力
檢視自我應考實力並提升考試臨場反應力

U0057230

作者序　Editor

　　在雅思考試的聽、說、讀、寫四部分中，聽力是一項透過恰當的練習，就可以在短時間內得到較高分數的單項。本書希望藉由字彙拓展、題型分析、和對話練習，幫助備考者快速提高聽力成績。

　　本書的字彙部份選取了 42 個雅思聽力考試可能會出現的情境，如租屋、旅行、大學課程等，整理出高頻場景中的主題字彙表，這一部分也可作為範例，由讀者來撰寫自己的主題字彙表，錙銖積累，擴大字彙量。題型部份擷取了劍橋雅思 7～10 中的範例，著重解析雅思聽力考試中的 6 種主要題型和各種類型的解題技巧。對話練習則是以日常簡易對話為主，做 Shadowing 練習，提升專注力。篇末附有兩份雅思聽力模擬試題以方便讀者做自我檢驗。

　　希望本書可以對雅思聽力的提高有所裨益。而在各種應試技巧之外，持之以恆、循序漸進的聽力訓練才是英文聽力能力進階的關鍵。

武董

編者序　Preface

　　雅思聽力不同於以往大家所熟悉的傳統聽力考試，設計上題型多變，不全為選擇題甚至整場考試下來，將近 30 題均為填空題。此一設計除了避免了考生是猜對答案，更能測出考生的英文拼字等能力。再者，雅思聽力前兩部分（Section1 和 Section2）為生活情景，而後兩部分為（Section3 和 Section4）為學術場景，能評鑑出考生到國外實際語言使用能力。也因為如此即使對於聽力良好的考生或於其他英語測驗拿到高分的考生來說，仍須熟悉生活和學術情景的字彙，因為這些都影響著考生是否能獲取高分。

　　此書設計的考生群為雅思聽力成績 5～7.5 左右的考生，考生可由書籍 Part1 中精選的常見雅思聽力字彙表背誦聽力中常考字彙。編輯部也於 Part2 規劃了雅思聽力常考題型，由劍橋雅思 7～10 中出現的題型作解說，考生能由 Part2 熟悉各個題型的答題技巧。

　　Part3 則是極其重要的一環，考生須破除看機經、寫劍橋雅思真題、聽力技巧的掌握等可立即提升雅思考試成績的迷思。**聽力的關鍵仍在於專注力（Concentration）和聽力理解力（Listening Comprehension）**，其他部分只是錦上添花而已。考生仍須花時間提升自己聽英文時的專注力和理解力，才是正確的方式。Part3 由幾個口譯技巧的搭配，shadowing（跟讀）、recall（回想）、C-E（中翻英）和E-C（英翻中），達到提升聽力專注力與口譯能力，考生除了書中提供的練習之外，可以由歐美影集或劍橋雅思真題 1～10（建議 7～10）聽力音檔練習聽力專注力。

　　最後書中提供了兩回模擬試題，試題中選了常見的雅思聽力話題，考生可以由此兩次測驗評估自己的應考實力，最後祝考生都能獲取理想成績。

編輯部敬上

目次 Contents

Part 1 必考字彙表 ● ● ●

Part **2** 答題技巧 ● ● ●

Part **3** 口譯練習 ● ● ●

Part 4 模擬試題 ● ● ●

Part 1
必考字彙表

Part 1 必考字彙表
Unit 1 常考話題 A

Topic 1 租屋概況

在租屋時，**房東**（landlord）會與**房客**（tenant）簽訂合約（contract）。簽約有時要透過**房屋仲介**（real estate agent），有時則是房東與房客談妥後自行簽訂。簽約時需要支付**押金**（deposit/bond），押金金額一般為一到三個月**租金**（rent）。付款則多為採取按月支付的方式（monthly payment）。很多學生選擇居住在**寄宿家庭**（homestay），以得到更好的照料；更多人選擇與人合租（share house），這樣生活更為獨立。除了租住一般的房屋，還可以選擇**學生公寓**（student apartment），短期遊學的同學更可以住在飯店或**青年旅社**（youth hostel）。在租金高的城市，**合租房間**（share room）是一種節約開支的辦法，**室友**（share mates）分擔房間的租金，更加經濟划算。

重要字彙	
landlord	房東
tenant	房客
contract	合約
real estate agent	房仲

deposit	押金
rent	房租
monthly payment	月付
homestay	寄宿家庭
share house	合租房
student apartment	學生公寓
youth hostel	青年旅社
share room	合租屋
roommate	室友
延伸字彙	
single room	單人房
double room	雙人房
suite	套房
services apartment	飯店式公寓
townhouse	連棟屋
studio	具廚具和衛浴的單人房
lobby	大廳
courtyard	院子
loft	閣樓
ensuite	帶盥洗室的主臥房
bathroom	浴室
living room/lounge	起居室
garage	車庫
corridor	走廊
central heating	中央供暖
balcony	陽台

Part 1

Part 2

Part 3

Part 4

Topic 2 租屋的外在環境與交通

　　找房子時，房客聯繫房東詢問是否還有空房（vacancy）並預約（make appointment）、看房（house inspection）。房子的地點（location）是重要的考量因素，因為關係到就學和打工的方便度。一般來說住在市中心（downtown）相對比較貴，而住在郊區（suburbs）較為便宜。要考慮住家附近是否有方便的大眾交通工具（public transport），到距離最近的公車站（bus station）或地鐵站（subway/metro station）要步行幾分鐘。如果自己駕車，則要詢問是否有停車位（parking lot）。另外也要確認住家與醫院（hospital）、學校（university）、超市（supermarket）的距離。簽約時要註明租住時長（duration），多久續租一次（renew the lease），何時可以入住（move in），以及開始付房租的時間。

重要字彙	
vacancy	空房
make an appointment	預約
house inspection	看房
location	地點
downtown	市中心；澳洲又稱 CBD (Central Business District)
suburb	郊區
public transport	大眾交通
bus station	公車站
subway/metro station	地鐵站
parking lot	停車位
hospital	醫院

university	大學
supermarket	超市
duration	時長
renew the lease	續租
move in	入住

延伸字彙

neighbourhood	附近環境
underground car park	地下停車位
uncovered car park	露天停車位
leasing office	公寓管理處
stairs	樓梯
lift	電梯
basement	地下室
lawn	草坪
fire exit	安全出口
gym	健身房
outdoor swimming pool	室外游泳池
terrace	露台
utility room	儲藏室

Part 1

Part 2

Part 3

Part 4

Topic 3 租屋的傢俱與電器

　　有的房子有附帶傢俱（furnished）和電器（white goods），可以詢問房東房子有提供（provide）什麼傢俱電器。一般情況下，即使是不帶傢俱的房子（unfurnished），房間也會提供基本的生活設施如廚房（kitchen）裡的煤氣灶（gas stove）或電磁灶（electricity stove）、嵌入式烤箱（build-in oven）、排氣扇（kitchen ventilator）、洗碗機（dishwasher）等，房間也自帶儲物空間如壁櫥（cupboard）和衣櫥（wardrobe），盥洗室的盥洗設備（shower/bath）也會齊備。一些房間安裝了空調（air conditioner），另一些則是吊扇（ceiling fan）。搬入不帶傢俱的房子，就需要房客自己採購需要的傢俱和電器，例如床墊（mattress）、沙發（sofa）、茶几（tea/coffee table）、餐桌（dinning table）、電視機（TV set）、冰箱（refrigerator）、洗衣機（washing machine）、烘乾機（dryer）等。

重要字彙	
furnished	帶傢俱
white goods	電器
provide	提供
unfurnished	不帶傢俱
kitchen	廚房
gas stove	煤氣灶／爐，瓦斯爐
electricity stove	電磁灶／爐
build-in oven	嵌入式烤箱
kitchen ventilator	廚房排氣扇
dishwasher	洗碗機

cupboard	壁櫥
wardrobe	衣櫥
shower/bath	盥洗設備
air conditioner	空調
ceiling fan	吊扇
mattress	床墊
sofa	沙發
tea/coffee table	茶几
dinning table	餐桌
TV set	電視機
refrigerator	電冰箱
washing machine	洗衣機
dryer	烘乾機
延伸字彙	
stereo system	音響設備
freezer	冷凍庫
kettle	電燒水壺
sink	洗碗池／洗臉槽
DVD player	DVD 播放器
stool	高腳椅
book cabinet	書櫃

Part 1
Part 2
Part 3
Part 4

Topic 4 租屋的開銷和注意事項

　　需要和房東確定租金是否包含水電費（including utilities），有時房客需要自費各種帳單（bills）如電（electricity）、水、網路（internet）、電話（telephone）、有線電視（cable TV）等費用。房客一般無須負擔市政管理費（council rates）和物業管理費（body cooperate fee/property management fee）。房東會負擔房屋裝修（renovation）和屋內設施（facilities）的維修服務（maintenance services），如果由房客墊付，則保留發票（invoice）或收據（receipt）之後向房東請款。如果入住公寓，也須確認是否禁止吸菸（no smoking）或禁養寵物（no pets）。一般大樓都有保全系統（security system），房客保管好自己的房門鑰匙（door key）或門禁卡（door card）就可以。洗衣則在自助洗衣房（laundromat）使用投幣式洗衣機（coin operated laundry machine）。

重要字彙	
including utilities	租金包含其他費用
bills	帳單
electricity	電
internet	網路
telephone	電話
cable TV	有線電視
council rates	市政管理費
body cooperate fee/property management fee	物業管理費
renovation	房屋裝潢
facilities	設施

maintenance services	維修服務
invoice	發票
receipt	收據
no smoking	禁止吸菸
no pets	禁養寵物
security system	保全系統
door key	房門鑰匙
door card	門禁卡
laundry	自助洗衣房
coin operated laundry machine	投幣式洗衣機
延伸字彙	
radiator	電暖爐
microwave	微波爐
toaster	烤麵包機
table lamp	檯燈
vacuum cleaner	吸塵器
water heater	熱水器
water dispenser	飲水機
mail box	信箱
curtain	窗簾

Part 1

Part 2

Part 3

Part 4

Topic 5 參觀藝術展

　　來到新的城市，美術館（art gallery）和博物館（museum）是一定要參觀的目的地（destination）。展廳中的雕塑（sculpture）和畫作（painting）令人想像力（imagination）飛馳。博物館的豐富館藏（collection）更是學習的最佳素材。倘徉在藝術的海洋中，人文精神和美感意識（aesthetics）都會得到滋養（nourishment）。展覽（exhibition）由主辦方（host）策劃多樣的主題（theme）。入場（admission）後，透過展廳平面圖（floor plan）獲得展品的大致位置。每一件展品（exhibit）都附有作品說明（label），更可以用租來的語音導覽（audio guide）獲得展品的詳細訊息。結束藝術館之旅後，可以在紀念品店（gift shop）買到展覽的周邊商品（merchandise）和明信片（post card）。

重要字彙	
art gallery	美術館
museum	博物館
destination	目的地
sculpture	雕塑
painting	畫作
imagination	想像力
collection	館藏
aesthetics	美感意識
nourishment	滋養
exhibition	展覽
host	主辦方
theme	主題

admission	入場
floor plan	平面圖
exhibit	展品
label	作品說明
audio guide	語音導覽
gift shop	紀念品店
merchandise	周邊商品
post card	明信片

延伸字量

architecture	建築
treasure	珍寶
display	陳列
visual art	視覺藝術
performance art	表演藝術
decorative art	裝飾藝術
textiles	紡織品
drawings	圖畫
photographs	攝影作品

Part 1

Part 2

Part 3

Part 4

Topic 6 參觀國家公園

　　國家公園（national park）是為了保護（conservation）生態而劃定的區域，最早和最知名的國家公園是美國的黃石國家公園（Yellowstone National Park）。國家公園多為自然生態保護區（protected areas），一定要確保遊玩時遵守景區的規定（regulation），協助生態保育（ecological conservation）。遊客可以自由設計興趣點（points of interest/POI），客製化（customized）自己的行程。 國家公園的景點（scene spots）包含各種地貌（landform），如山巒（mountain）、瀑布（waterfall）、峭壁（cliff）、火山（volcano）、海灘（beach）、湖泊（lake）等。可以透過書籍和網路得到旅行攻略（tour suggestion/travelling guide）。交通（transportation）和住宿（accommodation）是制定旅行計畫（travel plan）的要點，許多人選擇露營（camping）以更好親近自然。由於是戶外旅行，天氣（weather）狀況也要列入考慮。

重要字彙	
national park	國家公園
conservation	保護
Yellowstone National Park	黃石國家公園
protected areas	保護區，澳洲又稱 sanctuary
regulation	規定
ecological conservation	生態保育
points of interest/POI	興趣點
customised	客製化
scene spots	景點
landform	地貌

mountain	山巒
waterfall	瀑布
cliff	峭壁
volcano	火山
beach	海灘
lake	湖泊
tour suggestion/traveling guide	旅行攻略
transportation	交通
accommodation	住宿
travel plan	旅行計畫
camping	露營
weather	天氣

延伸字彙

visitor	遊客
outdoor recreation	戶外休閒
natural wonders	自然奇蹟
species	種群
habitat	棲息地
exploration	探索
prohibition	禁令
wilderness	荒野

Part 1

Part 2

Part 3

Part 4

Topic 7 參觀雪梨歌劇院

　　雪梨歌劇院（Sydney Opera House）是雪梨市的標誌性建築（landmark building）。曾被聯合國教科文組織（UNESCO / United Nations Educational Scientific and Cultural Organization）評為世界文化遺產（world cultural heritage）。歌劇院特別的貝殼（shell）造型搭配作為背景的港灣大橋（Sydney Harbor Bridge），吸引無數遊客來參觀。雪梨歌劇院的兩個主要演出場館（performance venues）分別是音樂廳（concert hall）和劇場（drama theatre），另外還有一些小劇場（playhouse）和多功能工作室（studio），其中音樂廳內有世界最大的機械管風琴（organ）。雪梨歌劇院外主要入口的前庭（forecourt）時常舉辦免費的公共演出（public performance）。除了用作觀光，歌劇院時常有歌劇（opera）、芭蕾舞劇（ballet）、音樂會（concert）等演出。

重要字彙	
Sydney Opera House	雪梨歌劇院
landmark building	標誌性建築
UNESCO	聯合國教科文組織
world cultural heritage	世界文化遺產
shell	貝殼
Sydney Harbour Bridge	雪梨港灣大橋
performance venues	演出場館
concert hall	音樂廳
drama theatre	劇場
playhouse	小劇場
studio	工作室

organ	管風琴
forecourt	前庭
public performance	公共演出
opera	歌劇
ballet	芭蕾舞劇
concert	音樂會
延伸字彙	
recording studio	錄音室
symphony orchestra	交響樂團
backstage	後台
art centre	藝術中心
structure	結構
audience	觀眾
foyer	門廳
conference	會議
ceremony	儀式
community event	社區活動
entrance	入口
fire exit	逃生出口

Part 1

Part 2

Part 3

Part 4

Topic 8 遊覽大堡礁

　　大堡礁（Great Barrier Reef）位於澳洲昆士蘭（Queensland）東北海岸，是全世界最大的珊瑚礁群（coral reef）。大堡礁由無數微小的珊瑚蟲（coral polyps）建構，整個海域蘊含豐富的海洋生物（marine life）。除了令人驚嘆的生物多樣性（bio-diversity），大堡礁數百座熱帶島嶼（tropical island）的美麗海灘（beach）吸引世界各地的遊客感受到自然的靈感（natural inspiration）。遊客在大堡礁可以體驗各種娛樂方式如浮潛（snorkeling）、潛水（scuba diving）、直升機旅行（helicopter tours）、郵輪之旅（cruise ship tours）、觀賞鯨魚（whale watching）、與海豚游泳（swimming with dolphins）等。大堡礁的當地文化是澳洲原住民（indigenous Australians / Australian aboriginal people）和托雷斯海峽島民（Torres Strait islander）文化，他們已經在澳洲土地上生活上萬年。

重要字彙	
Great Barrier Reef	大堡礁
Queensland	昆士蘭
coral reef	珊瑚礁
coral polyps	珊瑚蟲
marine life	海洋生物
bio-diversity	生物多樣性
tropical island	熱帶島嶼
beach	海灘
natural inspiration	自然的啟發
snorkelling	浮潛

scuba diving	潛水
helicopter tours	直升機旅行
cruise ship tours	郵輪之旅
whale watching	觀賞鯨魚
swimming with dolphins	與海豚游泳
indigenous Australian/Australian aboriginal people	澳洲原住民
Torres Strait islander	托雷斯海峽島民
延伸字彙	
pastime	休閒
scenic	風景秀美的
rainforest	熱帶雨林
the seven wonders of the natural world	世界七大自然奇蹟
exotic	奇異的
unspoilt	未遭破壞的
resort	度假地
ocean view	海景
sailing vessels/yachts	帆船
inshore	近海的
coast	海岸
coastal town	海濱小鎮
estuary	河口

Topic 9 訂機票

　　訂機票（book flight）可以透過旅行社（travel agency），也可以直接在航空公司（airline）的網頁預訂（reservation）。如果是網上直接預訂，第一步先填入基本資訊如出發地（origin）、目的地、單程（one way）或往返（return）票、出發日期（depart date）、返回日期、人數等。選擇合適航班後填入乘客信息（passenger details），選擇座位（seats），最後用信用卡（credit card）付款。選擇廉價航空公司（LCC/Low-cost Carrier）做短途飛行是節約開支的好辦法，許多廉航有嚴格的行李限制，登機箱（carry-on luggage）之外的托運行李（checked baggage）要另外購買，也不提供飛機餐。一般的航空公司會不定期推出如機票折扣（discount）的優惠（promotion），而提前預訂（book in advance）通常相對划算。

重要字彙	
book flight	訂機票
travel agency	旅行社
airline	航空公司
reservation	預訂
origin	出發地
one way	單程
return	往返
depart date	出發日期
passanger details	乘客信息
seats	座位
credit card	信用卡

LCC/Low-cost Carrier	廉價航空公司
carry-on luggage	登機箱
checked baggage	托運行李
discount	折扣
promotion	優惠
book in advance	提前預訂
延伸字彙	
economy class	經濟艙
business class	商務艙
upgrade	升等
confirm	確認
cancel	取消
window seat	靠窗的位子
aisle seat	靠走道的位子
suitcase	手提箱
fare	票價
check in	辦理登機手續
flight number	航班編號
handbag tag	行李牌

Part 1

Part 2

Part 3

Part 4

Topic 10 在機場出境

　　出國旅行應至少在飛機起飛前兩小時到達機場（airport）。首先要攜帶機票和護照（passport）在航空公司櫃台報到（check in），並辦理行李托運。離開報到櫃檯前要確認行李已經通過了機場的 X 光檢查（X-ray inspection）。安全稽查（passenger clearance）要求乘客走過安全門（security gate），以檢查是否攜帶違禁物品（prohibited items）。登機行李中的液體（liquid）體積不得超過 100ml。海關（customs）檢查護照之後可以在機場免稅店（duty-free shop）購買免稅商品（duty-free items）。大的國際機場有時需要到不同的航廈（terminal）登機，所以要確保在登機時間（boarding time）之前來到航班的登機門（boarding gate）。

重要字彙	
airport	機場
passport	護照
check in	報到
X-ray inspection	X 光檢查
passenger clearance	安全稽查
security gate	安全門
prohibited items	違禁物品
liquid	液體
customs	海關
duty-free shop	免稅店
duty-free items	免稅商品
terminal	航廈
boarding time	登機時間

boarding gate	登機門
延伸字彙	
flight duration	飛行時間
travel mileage	飛行里程
take off	起飛
landing	降落
itinerary	旅行日程表
departure lounge	候機室
delayed	延誤
boarding pass	登機證
transit	過境
domestic departure	國內航班出站
international departure	國際航班出港
goods to declare	報關物品
transfer passengers	轉機旅客
tax return	退稅
currency exchange	貨幣兌換處
arrival	入境
departure	離境

Topic 11 在機場入境

　　飛機降落前，空服員（flight attendant）會請乘客填寫入境申請表（disembarkation card/immigration form）以及海關申報表（customs declaration form）。入境後先做護照、簽證（visa）查驗，去行李提領區（baggage claim area）領取行李，海關檢查行李（baggage inspection）後即可抵達入境大廳（arrivals hall）。入境一個國家前，最好提前對需要申報（declare）的檢疫物品（quarantine items）做了解。譬如澳洲是入關檢疫非常嚴格的國家，如果沒有申報或丟棄（dispose）檢疫物品，則可能被罰款（fine）甚至被起訴（prosecuted）。機場的訊息中心（information center）提供所在城市的各種資訊。遊客可以攜帶國際駕照（international drivers license）前往租車處（car rental）租車，也可以乘坐機場巴士（airport bus）或接駁巴士（shuttle bus）前往目的地。

重要字彙	
flight attendant	空服員
disembarkation card/ immigration form	入境申請表
customs declaration form	海關申報表
visa	簽證
baggage claim area	行李提領區
baggage inspection	檢查行李
arrivals hall	入境大廳
declare	申報
quarantine items	檢疫物品

dispose	丟棄
fine	罰款
prosecuted	被起訴
information centre	訊息中心
international drivers licence	國際駕照
car rental	租車
airport bus	機場巴士
shuttle bus	接駁巴士

延伸字彙

luggage cart	行李推車
captain	機長
co-pilot	副駕駛
jet lag	時差症候群
meeting point	會面地點
life preserver	救生衣
ticket office	購票處
luggage locker	行李寄存處
escalator	自動扶梯
transfer correspondence	轉機處
scheduled time	預計時間
VIP room	貴賓室
taxi pick-up point	計程車乘車點
life jacket/vest	救生衣

Part 1

Part 2

Part 3

Part 4

Topic 12 藥店買藥

　　在藥店（pharmacy）可以直接購得非處方藥物（OTC drugs/over-the-counter drugs）；而購買處方藥物（prescription drugs）則必須憑醫生開具的處方（prescription/Rx）。處方上記載了病人的姓名、年齡、藥品名稱（drug name）、劑量（dosage）等，是藥劑師（pharmacist）向病人發放（dispense）藥品等重要依據。常用藥品如感冒藥（cold medicine）、止痛藥（painkiller）、非類固醇類消炎藥（NASID/non-steroidal anti-inflammatory drug）通常擺放在藥店顯眼位置。除了販賣藥品（medication/medicine），藥店也出售保健食品（healthy food）、化妝品（cosmetics）、皮膚護理品（skin care）等商品。如各種維他命（vitamins）、嬰兒配方奶粉（baby formula）、香水（fragrance）、糖果（confectionary）、牙齒保健品（dental care）。大的藥店會提供全部商品目錄（catalogue），以便消費者找到需要的產品。

重要字彙	
pharmacy	藥店
OTC drugs/over-the-counter drugs	非處方藥物
prescription drugs	處方藥
prescription/Rx	處方
drug name	藥品名
dosage	劑量
pharmacist	藥劑師
dispense	發放
cold medicine	感冒藥

painkiller	止痛藥
NASID/non-steroidal anti-inflammatory drug	非類固醇類消炎藥
medication/medicine	藥品
healthy food	保健食品
cosmetics	化妝品
skin care	皮膚護理品
vitamins	維他命
baby formula	嬰兒配方奶粉
fragrance	香水
confectionary	糖果
dental care	牙齒護理
catalogue	目錄
延伸字彙	
hair care	頭髮保養
protein	蛋白質
weight loss	減肥
fish oil	魚油
baby care	嬰兒用品
best sellers	暢銷商品
scar treatment	祛疤
cleansers	潔膚品

Part 1

Part 2

Part 3

Part 4

Topic 13 露營

　　露營（camping）是對環境友善（environmental friendly）的旅遊方式。不僅可以親近自然，而且低碳（LC/low carbon）節能（energy saving）。由於是露天居住，露營前一定要注意天氣的變化。另外也要選擇安全的露營區（campsite）。過夜用的裝備有睡袋（sleeping bag）、地墊（floor mat）和帳篷（tent）。露營天數越多，就需要攜帶越多的裝備（equipment）。租用露營車（recreational vehicle/motor caravan）駐紮在有清潔水源的空間是另一種露營方式。戶外野餐（picnic）也很有樂趣，可以用冷飲保藏盒（chest cooler/esky）攜帶準備好的食物，或用便攜式瓦斯爐（camp stove）烹飪簡單的食物。為了應對戶外過夜，也要準備必要的取暖和照明設備，如露營燈（camp lantern）手電筒（flashlight/torch）等。

重要字彙	
camping	露營
environmental friendly	環境友善
LC/low carbon	低碳
energy saving	節能
campsite	露營區
sleeping bag	睡袋
floor mat	地墊
tent	帳篷
equipment	裝備
recreational vehicle/motor caravan	露營車

picnic	野餐
chest cooler/esky	冷飲保藏盒
camp stove	便攜式瓦斯爐
camp lantern	露營燈
flashlight/torch	手電筒
延伸字彙	
camp fire	營火
compass	指南針
firewood	柴火
lighter	打火機
lime powder	石灰粉
backpack	背包
head torch	頭頂燈
foldable chair	折疊椅
travel pillow	旅行枕頭
first aid kit	急救箱
hike pot	野餐鍋
vacuum bullet flask	真空保溫瓶
accessories	附加裝備
umbrella	雨傘

Part 1

Part 2

Part 3

Part 4

Topic 14 遊覽澳洲動物園

　　澳洲動物園（Australia Zoo）位在昆士蘭的陽光海岸（Sunshine Coast），隔壁的澳洲動物園野生動物醫院（Australian Zoo Wildlife Hospital）以救護受傷動物而知名。遊客可以在澳洲動物園觀賞到各種鳥類、哺乳動物（mammals）和爬行動物（reptiles），體驗親手餵食大象（hand-feed elephants），觀賞鱷魚（crocodile）表演等。澳洲動物園的特色之一是遊客能夠近距離接觸許多動物（animal encounters），除了相對溫馴的袋鼠（kangaroo）和無尾熊（koala），還可以在工作人員（staff）的協助下接近更多野生動物（wildlife）如老虎、澳洲野狗（dingo）、巨型陸龜（giant tortoise）、長頸鹿（giraffe）、犀牛（rhinoceros）和獵豹（cheetah）。

重要字彙	
Australia Zoo	澳洲動物園
Sunshine Coast	陽光海岸
Australian Zoo Wildlife Hospital	澳洲動物園野生動物醫院
mammals	哺乳動物
reptiles	爬行動物
hand-feed elephants	親手餵食大象
crocodile	鱷魚
animal encounters	近距離接觸動物
kangaroo	袋鼠
koala	無尾熊
staff	工作人員
wildlife	野生動物

dingo	澳洲野狗
giant tortoise	巨型陸龜
giraffe	長頸鹿
rhinoceros	犀牛
cheetah	獵豹
延伸字彙	
camel	駱駝
possum	袋貂
Tasmania Devils	塔斯馬尼亞惡魔
wombat	毛鼻袋鼠
ibis	朱鷺
lizard	蜥蜴
venomous snake	毒蛇
vertebrates	脊椎動物
ectothermic	冷血動物
region	地帶
species	物種
forelimb	前肢

Topic 15 申請澳洲的手機門號

　　最方便的辦理手機門號方法是購買預付卡（pre-paid SIM card），這種門號不需要帶護照去特定的電信公司辦理，在便利商店（convenience store）或超商（supermarket）櫃台就可以購買。用預付卡是打完 SIM 卡中的額度再儲值（recharge），不含月租費（monthly fee），但卡上金額一般兩個月就會過期（expire），如果不繼續儲值門號就會消失。預付卡的通話費率較高，適合短期造訪的人使用。大多數人則是辦理綁約月租卡（post-paid Card），需要向電信公司提供身分證明（proof of identity），選擇手機型號和通話月租型方案（monthly plan），綁約時最好根據自己的需要選擇合適的話費和資料流量方案（data plan），因為更改資費方案一般要付一筆違約金（cancelation fee）。

重要字彙	
pre-paid SIM card	預付卡
convenience store	便利商店
supermarket	超商
recharge	儲值
monthly fee	月租費
expire	過期
post-paid card	月租卡
proof of identity	身分證明
monthly plan	月租型方案
data plan	資料流量方案
cancelation fee	違約金

延伸字彙	
voice message	語音留言
SMS	簡訊
smartphone	智慧型手機
HD camera	高畫素相機
bluetooth	藍牙
touch screen	觸控式螢幕
signal	手機訊號
ringtone	鈴聲
national call	國內通話
international call	國際通話
activate	開通
land line	市內電話
hash key	井字鍵
data usage	資料使用量
add-ons	增加
credit	基本額度
bonus	附贈額度
flag fall	接通費

Topic 16 在澳洲申請銀行帳戶

澳洲銀行帳戶主要有和銀行卡（bank card）綁定的存取帳戶（access account）和可以領到利息（interest）的儲蓄帳戶（saving account）。其中儲蓄帳戶的錢必須轉入存取帳戶裡才能動用。在每間銀行開戶都是這兩個帳戶系統，只是在名稱上有所差異。如聯邦銀行（Commonwealth Bank）的這兩個帳戶叫做主帳戶（complete access）和網路子帳戶（net bank saver）。銀行開戶手續非常簡單，只需攜帶護照去任意分行（branch）辦理。一定要將稅號（tax file number）提交給銀行，否則利息將被扣去一半。開戶後拿到的提款卡一般是簽帳金融卡（debit card），除在 ATM 領錢和線上刷卡外，平常可以買東西直接扣款（EFTPOS/electronic funds transfer at point of sale），也可以在買東西的櫃台提款（cash out），超市、便利店等收銀機都支持提款功能。

重要字彙	
bank card	銀行卡
access account	存取帳戶
interest	利息
saving account	儲蓄帳戶
Commonwealth Bank	聯邦銀行
complete access	主帳戶
net bank saver	網路子帳戶
branch	分行
tax file number	稅號
debit card	簽帳金融卡
EFTPOS/electronic funds transfer at point of sale	直接扣款

cash out	提款
延伸字彙	
BSB	銀行分行代號
transfer	轉帳
internet banking	網路銀行
account balance	帳戶餘額
cheque	支票
PIN	銀行卡密碼
payment	支付
credit	信用額度
money order	匯款單
security code	客戶服務密碼
account service fee	帳戶管理費
deposit	存款
transaction	交易
teller	銀行櫃員
foreign exchange rate	匯率
ATM/automatic teller machine	自動提款機
bank statement	銀行帳單

Part 1

Part 2

Part 3

Part 4

Topic 17 診所看病

在澳洲，若不是緊急狀況（emergency），生病後一般不是去醫院（hospital）看病，而是先要去診所（clinic）報到。在診所工作的是全科醫師／家醫師（GP/general practitioner），GP 會了解病人的身體狀況，如果是不嚴重的常見病如感冒（cold）、流感（flu）、發燒（fever）、外傷（wound）等，經驗良好的全科醫師就可以處理。如果需要進一步診斷檢查（diagnostic examination）或症狀是診所無法處理的，GP 會寫介紹信（refer letter）給專科醫師（medical specialist）做進一步診斷。許多 GP 提供診費全額報銷（bulk billing），如果是留學生使用海外醫療保險（overseas health cover），則需要先自費，再向健康保險公司（health insurance company）申請退款（refund）。

重要字彙	
emergency	緊急狀況
hospital	醫院
clinic	診所
GP/general practitioner	全科醫師
cold	感冒
flu	流感
fever	發燒
wound	外傷
diagnostic examination	診斷檢查
refer letter	介紹信
medical specialist	專科醫師
bulk billing	全額報銷

overseas health cover	海外醫療保險
health insurance company	健康保險公司
refund	退款
延伸字彙	
physician	內科醫生
allergy	過敏
nurse	護士
patient	病人
injection	打針
appetite	食慾
medical certificate	診斷書
laboratory	實驗室
ambulance	救護車
acupuncture	針灸
blood pressure	血壓
temperature	體溫
pulse rate	心率

Part 1
Part 2
Part 3
Part 4

Topic 18 看牙醫

去牙醫診所（dental clinic）看診前一般需要先預約（make an appointment），若非緊急情況，很少牙醫診所可以隨時入內看病（walk-in service）。打電話給牙醫診所後，診所櫃台人員（medical receptionist）會詢問姓名、生日（DOB/date of birth）和預約的原因，如有症狀（symptom）須簡單告知，並在診所提供的可預約時段（available time）選擇合適時間前往。如果是常規牙齒保健，牙醫（dentist）會檢查（check-up）牙齒並做洗牙和拋光（clean and polish）；如果是因為牙痛（toothache）看牙醫，則需要檢查是否有蛀牙（dental decay）、膿腫（abscess）、牙齒缺口（chipped tooth）等問題。再根據牙齒的狀況做拔牙（tooth extraction）、補牙（fillings）、根管治療（root canal therapy）、做牙冠（crown）等醫治（treatment）。

重要字彙	
dental clinic	牙醫診所
make an appointment	預約
walk-in service	隨時入內看病
medical receptionist	診所櫃台人員
DOB/date of birth	生日
symptom	症狀
available time	可預約時段
dentist	牙醫
check-up	檢查
clean and polish	洗牙和拋光
toothache	牙痛

dental decay	蛀牙
abscess	膿腫
chipped tooth	牙齒缺口
tooth extraction	拔牙
fillings	補牙
root canal therapy	根管治療
crown	牙冠
treatment	醫治

延伸字彙

hygienist	衛生保健專家
rinse the mouth	漱口
tongue	舌頭
gum	牙齦
cavity	蛀洞
brush the teeth	刷牙
nerves	神經
drill	鑽頭
anaesthesia	麻醉
floss	牙線

Part 1

Part 2

Part 3

Part 4

Topic 19 配眼鏡

　　視力（eyesight/vision）變差就需要去配眼鏡。配眼鏡一般先由驗光師（optometrist）檢查視力（eye check），許多眼鏡店（optical store）都提供免費的視力檢查。近視（myopia/short-sightedness）是最常見的眼科問題，驗光師指示念出圖表上的字母（letters on the chart）是測試單眼視力的方法。可以透過詳盡的視力檢查來診斷（diagnose）和評估（assessment）眼睛的（ocular）和視力問題。並配戴眼鏡（glasses）以功能性修復（functional repair）視力障礙（vision impairment）。如果驗光師判斷眼睛有更嚴重的問題需要進一步檢查，則會介紹病人去看眼科醫師（ophthalmologist/oculist）。驗光後挑選鏡片（lens/optic）和鏡架（frame）來配眼鏡，有些人則選擇配戴隱形眼鏡（contact lens）。

重要字彙	
eyesight/vision	視力
optometrist	驗光師
eye check	檢查視力
optical store	眼鏡店
myopia/short-sightedness	近視
letters on the chart	圖表上的字母
diagnose	診斷
assessment	評估
ocular	眼睛的
glasses	眼鏡
functional repair	功能性修復
vision impairment	視力障礙

ophthalmologist/oculist	眼科醫師
lens/optic	鏡片
frame	鏡架
contact lens	隱形眼鏡
延伸字彙	
corneal	角膜的
retina	視網膜
long-sighted	遠視
astigmia	散光
sunglasses	太陽眼鏡
reading glassed	花鏡
glasses' case	眼鏡盒
wlre frames	金屬眼鏡架
contact lens solution	隱形眼鏡護理液
optician	眼鏡商
scratch	（鏡片）刮花
oval frames	橢圓形眼鏡架
rectangular frames	長方形眼鏡架

Topic 20 看足科醫師

　　足踝醫學（podiatry）在許多國家是專門的學問，足踝（ankle）和腳掌（feet）的骨骼（bone）、關節（joint）和肌腱（muscle tendon）承受著身體全部重量，行走和跑步時則承重更多。足科醫師（podiatrist）幫助患者解決足踝和下肢（lower extremity）的病變，但治療技術和一般的骨科（orthopedics）不同。足科診所一般提供基本的足部保健（foot care），糖尿病足（diabetic foot）照護，兒童（pediatric）足科保健，器械矯正（orthotics）等。患者在足科診所可以做生物力學（biomechanics）和步態分析（gait analysis），做趾甲手術（nail surgery）；患有血管疾病（vascular disease）的高風險病人則可以做下肢感覺神經（sensory）的檢查。另外一些足部皮膚病（dermatitis）也可以得到治療，譬如香港腳（athlete foot）和皮膚真菌感染（fungal infection）。

重要字彙	
podiatry	足踝醫學
ankle	足踝
feet	腳掌
bone	骨骼
joint	關節
muscle tendon	肌腱
podiatrist	足科醫師
lower extremity	下肢
orthopaedics	骨科
foot care	足部保健
diabetic foot	糖尿病足

paediatric	兒童的
orthotics	器械矯正
biomechanics	生物力學
gait analysis	步態分析
nail surgery	趾甲手術
vascular disease	血管疾病
sensory	感覺神經
dermatitis	皮膚病
athlete foot	香港腳
fungal infection	真菌感染
延伸字彙	
plantar	足底
knee	膝關節
calf	小腿
thigh	大腿
spasm	痙攣
chiropody	足病治療

Part 1

Part 2

Part 3

Part 4

Topic 21 皇家農業展

　　皇家昆士蘭展覽會（Royal Queensland Show）又稱作 EKKA，是澳洲昆士蘭每年最大的節慶活動（festival），一般在八月份舉行。EKKA 成立的初衷是做農業（agricultural）展覽，由當地農夫（farmer）向外界展示新發明（invention）的農業機械（machinery）裝置（device）以及農場動物（farm animals）。舉辦超過百年的 EKKA 現在成為了展示本地文化（local culture）的視窗，吸引（attract）來到澳洲的外國遊客（foreign tourist）。農展會的有趣項目有露天遊樂場（fairground）、動物大遊行（animal parade）、伐木比賽（wood chopping competition）、馬術表演（equestrian）、煙火秀（firework）等。遊客也可以吃到展會上特別的零食（snack）像是棉花糖（fairy floss）、漢堡（burger）、熱薯條（hot chips），和最著名的草莓冰淇淋（strawberry sundae）。

重要字彙	
Royal Queensland Show	皇家昆士蘭展覽會
festival	節慶
agricultural	農業的
farmer	農夫
invention	發明
machinery	機械
device	裝置
farm animals	農場動物
local culture	本地文化
attract	吸引

foreign tourist	外國遊客
fairground	遊樂場
animal parade	動物人遊行
wood chopping competition	伐木比賽
equestrian	馬術表演
firework	煙火秀
snack	零食
fairy floss	棉花糖
burger	漢堡
hot chips	熱薯條
strawberry sundae	草莓冰淇淋
延伸字彙	
sideshow	雜耍
livestock	牲畜
poultry	家禽
paddock	訓馬場
boulevard	林蔭大道
pony	小馬
puppy	小狗

Topic 22 澳紐軍團日

　　澳紐軍團日（ANZAC day/Australian and New Zealand Army corps day）是為了紀念（commemorate）澳洲和紐西蘭在戰爭（war）、衝突（conflict）和維和行動（peacekeeping operation）中陣亡的軍人而創立的節日。軍團日是每年的 4 月 25 日。這個日子是澳紐軍團參加第一次世界大戰（the First World War）時，在土耳其（Turkey）的加里玻利（Gallipoli）海灘登陸（landing）的日子。在這次戰役（campaign）中，由於土耳其軍隊（army）的頑強抵抗（defense），澳紐軍團傷亡（casualty）慘重。戰事雖沒有取得勝利（triumph/victory），但陣亡的戰士給後人留下偉大的精神遺產（spiritual heritage），被稱作 ANZAC Legend 精神。現在人們以等待日出（sunrise）、軍樂隊（marching band）、老兵遊行（veteran parade）、紀念儀式（memorial）等來渡過這一節日。

重要字彙	
ANZAC day/Australian and New Zealand Army corps day	澳紐軍團日
commemorate	紀念
war	戰爭
conflict	衝突
peacekeeping operation	維和行動
the First World War	第一次世界大戰
Turkey	土耳其
Gallipoli	加里玻利
landing	登陸
campaign	戰役
army	軍隊

defence	抵抗
casualty	傷亡
triumph/victory	勝利
spiritual heritage	精神遺產
sunrise	日出
marching band	軍樂隊
veteran parade	老兵遊行
memorial	紀念儀式
延伸字彙	
revival	復興
national wide	全國
remembrance	紀念
contribution	貢獻
serve	服務
honour	榮譽
anniversary	紀念日
sovereign country	主權國家

Part 1

Part 2

Part 3

Part 4

Topic 23 大洋路

　　大洋路（Great Ocean Road）是澳洲維多利亞省（Victoria）南部的一條觀光公路（scenic route）。大洋路始建於 1919 年，以紀念第一次世界大戰中陣亡的士兵，是世界最大的戰爭紀念設施（war memorial）。公路沿海岸線（coastline）而建，沿途有漂亮的漁村（fishing village）、由石灰岩（limestone）和砂岩（sandstone）構成（composed）的懸崖和海灘、遼闊的雨林（rainforest）、有時還會遇到鯨魚（whale）遷徙（migrate）。大洋路上著名的景點十二門徒（Twelve Apostles）是岩石受到海潮（ocean tide）侵蝕（erosion）形成的景觀，人們用耶穌基督（Jesus Christ）的十二位弟子命名十二個巨型岩石柱。大洋路步行路線（Great Ocean walk）是專門為步行遊客設計的健行步道（hiking trail），遊客穿越國家公園，遊覽海洋保護區（marine reserve）的美景。

重要字彙	
Great Ocean Road	大洋路
Victoria	維多利亞省
scenic route	觀光公路
war memorial	戰爭紀念設施
coastline	海岸線
fishing village	漁村
limestone	石灰岩
sandstone	砂岩
composed	構成
rainforest	雨林
whale	鯨魚

migrate	遷徙
Twelve Apostles	十二門徒
ocean tide	海潮
erosion	侵蝕
Jesus Christ	耶穌基督
Great Ocean walk	大洋路步行路線
hiking trail	健行步道
marine reserve	海洋保護區
延伸字彙	
invaluable	無價的
rock fall	落石
eco-friendly	生態友好的
landscape	陸上風景
stretch	延伸
hike	遠足
rehabilitation	復原

Part 1

Part 2

Part 3

Part 4

Topic 23 考駕照

　　無論是在澳洲學習開車，還是把外國駕照（driver's licence）換成澳洲駕照，都必須通過電腦化（computerized）交通規則考試（road rules test）和路考（driving test）。交通規則考試是理論（theoretical）考試，檢驗受試者的交通安全（driving safety）常識，對交通規則和道路交通號誌（road traffic signals）的了解等安全知識。考試通過後獲得學習駕照（learner licence），持學習駕照行車必須有正式駕照（open licence）持有者監督（supervision），並按照要求紀錄行車日誌簿（logbook）。拿 L 牌超過一年並積累到 100 小時開車經驗後，就可以向當地交通部（transport department）申請參加路考。通過路考後，駕齡超過三年者可以得到正式駕照，不滿三年者則得到臨時駕照（provisional licence），需要再經過司機資格考試（driver qualification test）換正式駕照。（每個州制度略有差異）

重要字彙	
driver's licence	駕照
computerised	電腦化
road rules test	交通規則考試
driving test	路考
theoretical	理論
driving safety	交通安全
road traffic signals	道路交通號誌
learner licence	學習駕照
open licence	正式駕照
supervision	監督

logbook	日誌簿
transport department	交通部
provisional licence	臨時駕照
driver qualification test	司機資格考試
延伸字彙	
valid	有效
demerit point system	違規扣分制度
upgrade	升級
eligible	有資格的
speeding offence	超速
hazard	危險
perception	感知
alcohol limit	飲酒限量
restriction	限制
suspension	暫停
disqualification	取消資格
speed limit	限速

Part 1

Part 2

Part 3

Part 4

Topic 24 租車

　　澳洲幅員廣闊，租車（car rental）可以使旅行更加便利。有網路訂車、電話訂車或親臨訂車等方式，其中網路訂車時常會得到特殊優惠（concession）。租車過程（process）是選擇租車地點和車型（vehicle model）、確認租車價格（price）和包含的服務項目（services）、填寫個人資料和信用卡資料即可完成。租車一般推薦（recommend）購買全險（fully comprehensive coverage），需要和租車公司確認理賠費（excess fee），這部分是一旦發生意外，承租者先行負擔的部分，之後才由保險公司接手負擔。另外租車者的年齡如果未滿 25 歲，各種費用都會比較高。租車通例是滿油箱（full tank）租車滿油箱歸還，可以根據需要加租導航（GPS/Global Position System）、兒童安全座椅（child safety seat）等。

重要字彙	
car rental	租車
concession	優惠
process	過程
vehicle model	車型
price	價格
services	服務項目
recommend	推薦
fully comprehensive coverage	全險
excess fee	理賠費
full tank	滿油箱
GPS/Global Position System	導航
child safety seat	兒童安全座椅

延伸字彙	
unlimited kilometres	不限里程
vehicle registration	車輛註冊
airport tax	機場稅
damage	損毀
automatic	自動檔
manual	手排檔
A/C air-conditioning	空調
reservation	預訂
coupon	兌換點數
discount	折扣
hybrid vehicle	混合動力車
enhance	加強
budget	預算
refund	退款

Part 1

Part 2

Part 3

Part 4

Topic 25 澳洲高等教育

　　澳洲的高等教育（tertiary education）分為技術學院（TAFE/Technical And Further Education）和大學（university）兩類。技術學院主要提供技術性（technical）的課程，一般修習 2 至 3 年；大學則根據科系（faculty）不同學習 3 到 7 年不等。TAFE 的專業技術（professional skills）訓練偏重實際運用（practical application），對職業發展（career development）有具體幫助。大學學習比較專精，本科生（undergraduate）學習結束後獲得學士學位（Bachelor Degree）。有志學術（academic）者還可以繼續修讀碩士學位（Master Degree）和博士學位（Doctoral Awards）。其中碩士學位有研究型（Master by research）和修課型（Master by coursework）；博士學位則分為一般博士學位（Doctor of Philosophy）和針對專業領域的專業博士學位（ Professional Doctorate ）。

重要字彙	
tertiary education	高等教育
TAFE/Technical and Further Education	技術學院
university	大學
technical	技術性
faculty	科系
professional skills	專業技術
practical application	實際運用
career development	職業發展
undergraduate	本科生

Bachelor Degree	學士學位
academic	學術
Master Degree	碩士學位
Doctoral Awards	博士學位
Master by research	研究型碩士學位
Master by coursework	修課型碩士學位
Doctor of Philosophy	一般博士學位
Professional Doctorate	專業博士學位

延伸字彙

postgraduate	研究生
Honours Degree	榮譽學位
Combined Degrees/Double Degrees	雙學位
LLB/Bachelor of Laws	法學學士學位
MBBS/Bachelor of Medicine, Bachelor of Surgery	內外全科醫學學士
Graduate Certificate	碩士證書
Graduate Diploma	碩士文憑
PhD programme	碩博連讀
PhD candidate	博士候選人

　　澳洲的大學或研究所（graduate school）申請（application）可以透過留學代辦（education agent）辦理或自己直接申請。在確定好學校和課程（course）後，需要準備一些證明文件（supporting documents）：最高學歷的成績單（academic transcript）以及課程額外（additional）要求（requirements）的文件，像是設計系（School of Design）要求的作品（production/works）。或護理系（Faculty of Nursing）要求的註冊（registration）證照（licence）。證明文件必須是經過認證的副本（certified copies）。非英文母語國家的申請者需要提供英語水平（English language proficiency）證書（certificate），如雅思（IELTS）和托福（TOFEL）成績單。必須在截止日期（closing date）之前遞出申請。申請過程（process）一般需要一至四週，得到錄取通知書（offer）後，即可以安排機票住宿和申請學生簽證（student visa）。

重要字彙	
graduate school	研究所
application	申請
education agent	留學代辦
course	課程
supporting documents	證明文件
academic transcript	成績單
additional	額外
requirements	要求
School of Design	設計系
production/works	作品

Faculty of Nursing	護理系
registration	註冊
licence	證照
certified copies	經過認證的副本
English language proficiency	英語水平
certificate	證書
IELTS	雅思
TOFEL	托福
closing date	截止日期
process	過程
offer	錄取通知書
student visa	學生簽證
延伸字彙	
conditional/provisional offer	條件入學許可
preliminary program	大學預科
letter of rejection	拒絕信
scholarship	獎學金

Part 1

Part 2

Part 3

Part 4

Topic 27 正式入學前的英文進修

　　大學常有專門為海外學生（overseas students）開設的語言學校（language school）。方便英文尚未達到入學要求的學生做英文進修。語言學校開設的主要課程是普通英文（GE/General English）和學術英文（EAP/English for Academic Purposes）以及專門針對雅思考試的應試培訓等。普通英文課程重在提升交流（communication）能力，聽力（listening）、閱讀（reading）、寫作（writing）、字彙（vocabulary）都是主要練習的項目。學術英文則依據大學的學習要求培養進階的（advanced）英文能力：如報告（essay）和論文（assignment）寫作、學術引用（referencing）、課堂筆記（note-taking）和總結（summarizing）、專題研究（research）技巧、演講（presentation）、論文檢索（article search）等。這些英文訓練不僅幫助打好英文基礎（foundation），也對之後的學業大有裨益。

重要字彙	
overseas students	海外學生
language school	語言學校
GE/General English	普通英文
EAP/English for Academic Purposes	學術英文
communication	交流
listening	聽力
reading	閱讀
writing	寫作

vocabulary	字彙
advanced	進階的
essay	報告
assignment	論文
referencing	學術引用
note-taking	課堂筆記
summarising	總結
research	專題研究
presentation	演講
article search	論文檢索
foundation	基礎
進階字彙	
competence	能力
proficiency	熟練
word processing	文字處理
database	資料庫
library	圖書館
dictionary skills	辭書檢索能力
method	學習方法

Part 1

Part 2

Part 3

Part 4

Topic 28 大學的學習

　　正式開學前有迎新週（orientation week），新生來學校報到（enroll）和選課（select courses），聽取對專業（major）、學習方法（learning strategies）、課業任務（study load）的介紹（introduction）。課程可以自己選擇，除了專業必修課程（compulsory course）外還可以修讀選修課程（elective course）。普通課程包含講座（lecture）和輔導課（tutorial），講座一般是兩小時，由教授（professor）講解一章知識，輔導課則由導師（tutor）解決練習題（exercise）和課後學習的問題。一科大學課程通常需要（require）每週 10 到 12 小時的學習時間，全職學生（full-time student）一般會選擇每學期（semester）四或五門（unit）課程。大學是完全的自主（independent）學習，科目和上課時間都可以自己安排，只得到很少的指導（supervise）。

重要字彙	
orientation week	迎新週
enroll	報到
select courses	選課
major	專業
learning strategies	學習方法
study load	課業任務
introduction	介紹
compulsory course	必修課程
elective course	選修課程
lecture	講座
tutorial	輔導課

professor	教授
tutor	導師
exercise	練習題
require	需要
full-time student	全職學生
semester	學期
unit	門／科
independent	自主
supervise	指導
延伸字彙	
part-time student	兼職學生
semester break	假期
guideline	大綱
feedback	反饋
open day	開放日
institute	機構

Part 1

Part 2

Part 3

Part 4

Topic 29 大學的考核

　　撰寫學術報告（academic essay）是重要的考核（assessment）方式。學術報告一般比較簡短，且需要遵循學術寫作（academic writing）的規則，文章結構（structure）為緒論（introduction）、主要內容（body）和結論（conclusion）。為了撰寫報告需要大量閱讀，包括老師提供的參考書目（reading list）以及從資料庫檢索（retrieve）文章。報告的分數（score）會按照評分標準（marking criteria）給出。學期中會有個人演講（presentation）、小組作業（group work）、小測驗（quiz）等考核，每個項目都佔總成績的一定百分比（percentage）。一些科目的期末考試（final exam）則以寫論文（assignment）方式完成。其中理工科（science and engineering）學生需要撰寫實證性（empirical）研究論文（research paper），論文章節需要介紹研究方法、研究結果（result）和討論（discussion）。

重要字彙	
academic essay	學術報告
assessment	考核
academic writing	學術寫作
structure	結構
introduction	緒論
body	主要內容
conclusion	結論
reading list	參考書目
retrieve	檢索
score	分數
marking criteria	評分標準

presentation	演講
group work	小組作業
quiz	小測驗
percentage	百分比
final exam	期末考試
assignment	論文
science and engineering	理工科
empirical	實證性
research paper	研究論文
result	研究結果
discussion	討論
延伸字彙	
dissertation	學位論文
topic	主題
bibliographies	書目／文獻
proofreading	校對

Topic 30 大學的專業

　　澳洲的高等教育在許多學科（discipline）都達到國際先進水準，尤其是工程技術（engineering and technology）、醫學（medicine）、環境科學（environmental science）、會計金融（accounting and finance）等。有些學科則有高比例的學生修讀雙學位，譬如藝術（arts）、管理（management）、貿易（commerce）、法學（law）和健康科學（health science）。除了傳統的自然科學（natural science）和社會科學（social science）專業，澳洲大學的職業（professions）與應用科學（applied science）也有很高的教學品質，例如農業（agriculture）、建築（architecture）、教育（education）、新聞學（journalism）、傳播學（communication）、公共衛生（public health）、社會工作（social work）等。形式科學（formal science）方面也建樹頗豐，如計算機科學（computer science）、邏輯學（logic）、統計學（statistics）、數學（mathematics）。

重點字彙	
discipline	學科
engineering and technology	工程技術
medicine	醫學
environmental science	環境科學
accounting and finance	會計金融
arts	藝術
management	管理
commerce	貿易
law	法學
health science	健康科學

natural science	自然科學
social science	社會科學
professions	職業
applied science	應用科學
agriculture	農業
architecture	建築
education	教育
journalism	新聞學
communication	傳播學
public health	公共衛生
social work	社會工作
formal science	形式科學
computer science	計算機科學
logic	邏輯學
statistics	統計學
mathematics	數學
physics	物理學
chemistry	化學

Part 1

Part 2

Part 3

Part 4

Topic 31 大學的設施

　　大學的講座通常被安排在座位較多的階梯教室（lecture theatre），輔導課則在普通教室（classroom）。多媒體（multimedia）教室都配有白板（writing board）、計算機（computer）、投影儀（projector）、無線（wireless）擴音器（microphone）等設備（equipment）。圖書館（library）有公共電腦房（computer lab）、閱覽室（reference room）、自習室（individual study room），並提供拷貝（copy）和列印（printing）設施。除實體書外，也提供電子書（e-books）借閱服務。大學校園裡有書店（bookshop）、餐廳（canteen）、健身房（gym）、游泳池（swimming pool）、學校診所（school clinics）、藝術設施（art facilities）等。很多大學都設有幼兒中心（child care centre）和育嬰室（parenting room），以幫助有年幼小孩的學生。禱告室（preyer room）則為有宗教（religious）需要的學生提供空間。

重要字彙	
lecture theatre	階梯教室
classroom	教室
multimedia	多媒體
writing board	白板
computer	計算機
projector	投影儀
wireless	無線
microphone	擴音器
equipment	設備
library	圖書館

computer lab	電腦房
reference room	閱覽室
individual study room	自習室
copy	拷貝
printing	列印
e-books	電子書
bookshop	書店
canteen	餐廳
gym	健身房
swimming pool	游泳池
school clinics	學校診所
art facilities	藝術設施
child care centre	幼兒中心
parenting room	育嬰室
prayer room	禱告室
religious	宗教
campus	校園
security	安全

Part 1

Part 2

Part 3

Part 4

Topic 32 研究方法之量化研究

　　量化研究（quantitative research）是一種符合邏輯（logical）並以數據（data）為基礎的研究方法（methodology），被廣泛應用於自然科學和社會科學諸領域。是透過統計（statistical）、數學（mathematical）及計算（computational），對現象（phenomenon）進行考察（investigation）。研究者（researcher）做數據分析（data analyze），以期得到（yield）可以通用與大範圍人群（population）的公正結果（unbiased result）。完整的研究進程包括了研究設計（research design）、數據分析、及研究的效度（validity）與信度（reliability/credibility）等問題。取得資料後，要依據各種預測變數（predictor variable）和結果變數（outcome variable）的數量與性質採取不同的統計方法。如以類別變數（categorical variables）測比例（proportion）時用卡方檢定（Chi-square test）；以兩組連續變量（continuous variables）測標準誤差（standard deviation）用 T 檢定（T-test）；預測（prediction）和因果分析（causal analysis）則用線性回歸（linear regression）。

重要字彙	
quantitative research	量化研究
logical	邏輯
data	數據
methodology	方法
statistical	統計
mathematical	數學
computational	計算
phenomenon	現象

investigation	考察
researcher	研究者
data analyse	數據分析
yield	得到
population	人群
unbiased result	公正結果
research design	研究設計
validity	效度
reliability/credibility	信度
predictor variable	預測變數
outcome variable	結果變數
categorical variables	類別變數
proportion	比例
Chi-square test	卡方檢定
continuous variables	連續變量
standard deviation	標準誤差
T-test	T 檢定
prediction	預測
causal analysis	因果分析
linear regression	線性回歸

Topic 33 研究方法之質化研究

與量化研究相對，質化研究（qualitative research）專注在更小更集中（focused）的樣本（samples），透過個案研究（case study）得到的資訊（information），深入（in-depth）瞭解（understanding）人類行為（behavior）及其理由（reason）。質化研究常被運用於社會科學的眾領域。質化研究最常見的（popular）方法個案研究，是以經驗為主（empirical）的調查法來研究具體生活（real-life）。在個案研究所處理的獨特（unique）事件中，研究者可能對事件中的許多變數感興趣，因此需要依賴不同來源（sources）的證據（evidence）。不限於學術領域，公司（cooperation）企業也常利用個案研究法，常見的 SWOT 分析法包含了優勢（strength）、劣勢（weakness）、機會（opportunity）、威脅（threat）的分析，從正反兩面做綜合（comprehensive）分析，為決策制定（decision making）提供依據。

重要字彙	
qualitative research	質化研究
focused	集中
samples	樣本
case study	個案研究
information	資訊
in-depth	深入
understanding	瞭解
behaviour	行為
reason	理由
popular	常見的

empirical	以經驗為主
real-life	具體生活
unique	獨特
sources	來源
evidence	證據
cooperation	公司
strength	優勢
weakness	劣勢
opportunity	機會
threat	威脅
comprehensive	綜合
decision making	決策制定
延伸字彙	
sociology	社會學
plausible	貌似合理的
hypothesis	假設
proposition	主張，論點

Topic 34 校園就業服務

　　許多大學都提供就業（employment）輔導服務，以及特別針對國際學生（international student）的職業（career）諮詢（consultant）。高年級（senior grades）學生可以參加免費的（free）為就業做準備（preparation）的研討會（workshop），得到職業規劃（career planning）的建議（advice）和就業輔助（assistance）。一些大學甚至設有特別為幫助學生求職的導師（mentor）計畫（scheme），學生可以做面試（interview）練習（practice），修改簡歷（resume），模擬申請（application）工作。大學也會組織（organize）招聘會（recruitment fair），使學生有機會見到潛在（potential）雇主（employer）。透過學校的就業平台（platform），學生也可以得到更多的邁入業界（industry）的機會（opportunity），譬如應徵到兼職（part-time）工作、非正式（casual）工作，實習生（internship）和培訓生計畫（graduate program）。

重要字彙	
employment	就業
international student	國際學生
career	職業
consultant	諮詢
senior grades	高年級
free	免費的
preparation	準備
workshop	研討會
career planning	職業規劃
advice	建議

assistance	輔助
mentor	導師
scheme	計畫
interview	面試
practice	練習
resume	簡歷
application	申請
organize	組織
recruitment fair	招聘會
potential	潛在的
employer	雇主
platform	平台
Industry	業界
opportunity	機會
part-time	兼職
casual	非正式
internship	實習生
graduate program	培訓生計畫

Part 1

Part 2

Part 3

Part 4

Topic 35 求職

　　求職網站（job website）會發布雇主的徵人廣告（advertisement），只需鍵入職務名稱（job title）、自己的專長（skills）、工作地點或郵遞區號（postcode），就可以瀏覽（browse）符合條件的工作崗位。需要仔細閱讀職位說明（position description），尤其是工作任務描述（duty statement）和選拔準則（selection criteria）。許多崗位要求應徵者（applicant）在求職信（cover letter）中撰寫自己符合選拔準備的原因。簡歷（CV/resume）的書寫原則是簡潔扼要（concise），一般不超過兩頁紙，且應當注意拼寫（spelling）。人資部門（HR/human resource）對簡歷篩選（screen）後，會通過電話或電子郵件（e-mail）方式通知是否進入面試（interview）階段。專業社群網站（social network）LinkedIn 搭配應用軟體（application software），求職者可以上傳（upload）和編輯（edit）自己的專業履歷（professional CV），也可以獲得最新的行業資訊，也是最常用的求職網站。

重要字彙	
job website	求職網站
advertisement	廣告
job title	職務名稱
skills	專長
postcode	郵遞區號
browse	瀏覽
position description	職位說明
duty statement	任務說明
selection criteria	選拔準則
applicant	應徵者

cover letter	求職信
CV/resume	簡歷
concise	簡潔扼要
spelling	拼寫
HR/human resource	人資
screen	篩選
e-mail	電子郵件
interview	面試
social network	社群網站
application software	應用軟體
upload	上傳
edit	編輯
professional CV	專業履歷
延伸字彙	
recommendation	推薦
background	背景
profile	檔案

Part 1

Part 2

Part 3

Part 4

Topic 36 急救認證

　　安全急救（First Aid）認證（certificate）課程是被澳洲政府推廣（promote）在全國都被認可的（accredited）認證，無論從事何種工作都推薦參加這一訓練（training）。許多合法（legitimate）註冊的（registered）訓練機構（organization），如紅十字會（Red Cross）、救護車服務站（Ambulance Service）等都提供急救認證課程。在課程中學員可以習得職業健康安全（occupational health and safety）和危機處理（crisis management），了解緊急狀況發生時生命維持（life support）的支援方法。學習心肺復甦術（CPR/cardiopulmonary resuscitation）的知識和操作，意外受傷（injury）如扭傷（sprain）、脫臼（dislocation）、燒傷（burns）、脫水（dehydration）、中暑（heat stroke）、叮咬（bites/stings）、失血（bleeding）等狀況發生時，專業醫療介入前的簡單支援在學習範圍內。

重要字彙	
First Aid	安全急救
certificate	認證
promote	推廣
accredited	被認可的
training	訓練
legitimate	合法
registered	註冊的
organization	機構
Red Cross	紅十字會
Ambulance Service	救護車服務站

occupational health and safety	職業健康安全
crisis management	危機處理
life support	生命維持
CPR/cardiopulmonary resuscitation	心肺復甦術
injury	受傷
sprain	扭傷
dislocation	脫臼
burns	燒傷
dehydration	脫水
heat stroke	中暑
bites/stings	叮咬
bleeding	失血
延伸字彙	
cardiac conditions	心臟病
asthma	氣喘
fracture	骨折
loss of consciousness	失去知覺

Part 1

Part 2

Part 3

Part 4

Topic 37 袋鼠

　　袋鼠是彈跳力（jumping）最強的哺乳動物（mammal），是澳洲地方性的（endemic）動物。不同種類（species）的袋鼠分佈在不同的自然環境中，其中體型較大的一類被叫做袋鼠（kangaroo），體型較小的被稱為沙袋鼠（wallaby）。袋鼠有粗壯的後腿（hind legs）和大腳以適應跳躍（leaping），長尾巴（tail）則利於保持平衡（balance）。雌性（female）袋鼠像其他有袋動物（marsupials）一樣，腹部（abdomen）前開一個袋子（pouch），幼袋鼠（joey）就在袋子裡完成出生後（postnatal）的發育，直到能夠獨立適應外部生存再脫離母體。袋鼠是澳洲的國家象徵（symbol），和鴯鶓（emu）一起出現在澳洲國徽（coat of arms）上。澳航（Qantas）和澳洲皇家空軍（Royal Australian Air Force）也都將袋鼠作為標誌。

重要字彙	
jumping	彈跳力
mammal	哺乳動物
endemic	地方性的
species	種類
kangaroo	袋鼠
wallaby	沙袋鼠
hind legs	後腿
leaping	跳躍
tail	尾巴
balance	平衡
female	雌性

marsupials	有袋動物
abdomen	腹部
pouch	袋子
joey	幼袋鼠
postnatal	出生後
symbol	象徵
emu	鴯鶓
coat of arms	國徽
Qantas	澳航
Royal Australian Air Force	澳洲皇家空軍
延伸字彙	
habitat	棲息地
graze	放牧
predator	捕食者
arid	乾旱的
regurgitate	反芻

Topic 38 無尾熊

　　無尾熊（koala）也是澳洲特有的有袋動物，Koala 這個名稱來自於原住民方言（dialect），意思是 "不喝水"。無尾熊的唯一食物是尤加利樹（eucalyptus），樹葉（leaf）提供的足夠水分使無尾熊無須飲水。由於尤加利樹纖維（fiber）堅硬，營養（nutrition）和熱量（calories）很少，所以無尾熊必須保持靜止不動（sedentary）且每天睡眠超過 20 小時的生活模式（mode）。無尾熊新陳代謝（metabolism）緩慢，又需要耗費大量清醒時光進食，因而個體之間互動（interaction）極少，屬於非群居動物（asocial animal）。無尾熊顯著的（recognizable）特徵是體態肥胖（stout）、身體不長尾巴（tailless）、毛茸茸的（fluffy）耳朵和黑色的湯匙狀鼻子。它們性情溫順，抱無尾熊拍照是澳洲的動物園受歡迎的項目。

重要字彙	
koala	無尾熊
dialect	方言
eucalyptus	尤加利樹
leaf	樹葉
fiber	纖維
nutrition	營養
calories	熱量
sedentary	靜止不動
mode	模式
metabolism	新陳代謝
interaction	互動
asocial animal	非群居動物

recognisable	顯著的
stout	肥胖
tailless	不長尾巴
fluffy	毛茸茸的
延伸字彙	
woodlands	樹林
offspring	後代
subspecies	亞種
hairless	無毛的
belly	腹部
insulate	使隔絕
resilient	適應力強的
geographic range	地理分佈
cheek	臉頰
chubby	胖乎乎的

Part 1

Part 2

Part 3

Part 4

Topic 39 全球暖化

全球暖化（global warming）是由於溫室效應（Greenhouse effect）造成的全球平均氣溫（average temperature）逐漸（gradually）升高（increase）。全球暖化被認為會對地球氣候（climate）造成永久（permanent）改變。近地面（near-surface）大氣的（atmospheric）溫度升高和海洋（ocean）變暖在過去幾十年（decades）內呈現出前所未見的（unprecedented）趨勢。科學研究（scientific research）發現，導致全球暖化的主要原因是人類活動（human activities）排放的大量溫室氣體（greenhouse gases），如水蒸氣（vapour）、二氧化碳（carbon dioxide）、甲烷（methane）等。全球性的溫度增高使得海平面（sea level）上升和降水量（precipitation）增多，這進一步導致極端氣候（extreme weather）出現更加頻繁（frequent），發生更多的洪水（flood）、乾旱（drought）、熱帶氣旋（tropical cyclone），甚至影響農業（agriculture）、減少物種和加劇疾病傳播（spread）。

重要字彙	
global warming	全球暖化
Greenhouse effect	溫室效應
average temperature	平均氣溫
gradually	逐漸
increase	升高
climate	氣候
permanent	永久的
near-surface	近地面
atmospheric	大氣的
ocean	海洋

decades	幾十年
unprecedented	前所未見的
scientific research	科學研究
human activities	人類活動
greenhouse gases	溫室氣體
vapour	水蒸氣
carbon dioxide	二氧化碳
methane	甲烷
sea level	海平面
precipitation	降水量
extreme weather	極端氣候
frequent	頻繁
flood	洪水
drought	乾旱
tropical cyclone	熱帶氣旋
agriculture	農業
exacerbate	加劇
spread	傳播

Part 1

Part 2

Part 3

Part 4

Topic 40 土壤侵蝕退化

　　土壤（soil）是地球的肌膚（skin），土壤上充滿活力的（dynamic）生態系統（ecosystem）為人類和其他生物提供了生存空間（space）和資源（resource）。人口增多導致對農產品（agriculture commodities）需求量增大，許多森林（forest）和草場（grassland）被改為農地（farm field）和牧場（pasture）。農作物（crops）吸取土壤營養（nutrition），不像天然植被（natural vegetation）具有水土保持（conservation）的作用，土壤更容易被侵蝕（erosion）。在過去的 150 年裡，陸地上的表層土（topsoil）已經流失過半。除此之外，土壤品質（quality）也逐漸退化（degradation）。密集種植（intensive cultivation）和大量使用殺蟲劑（pesticide）加劇了土壤營養物質（nutrient）流失，造成土質固化（compaction）、鹽鹼化（salinity）。唯有土地的可持續（sustainable）利用才能阻止（prevent）土壤侵蝕退化。

重要字彙	
soil	土壤
skin	肌膚
dynamic	充滿活力的
ecosystem	生態系統
space	空間
resource	資源
agriculture commodities	農產品
forest	森林
grassland	草場
farm field	農地

pasture	牧場
crops	農作物
nutrient	營養物質
natural vegetation	天然植被
conservation	保持
erosion	侵蝕
topsoil	表層土
quality	品質
degradation	退化
intensive cultivation	密集種植
pesticide	殺蟲劑
compaction	固化
salinity	鹽鹼化
prevent	阻止
延伸字彙	
sustainable	可持續
fertile	肥沃的
pollution	污染
impact	影響

Topic 41 沙漠化

　　沙漠化（desertification）是土壤退化的一種型態。指土地失去水體（bodies of water）、表層植被（vegetation）和野生動物，變得乾旱（arid）貧瘠（barren）。導致沙漠化的直接（immediate）原因是植被流失，乾旱、砍伐森林（deforestation）、過度放牧（overgrazing）等都會導致沙漠化。沙漠化導致沙塵暴（sandstorm）增多、人類可利用的生活面積（area）減少、生態平衡（ecological equilibrium）也受到影響。人們目前掌握的技術可以減輕（mitigate）或逆轉（reverse）沙漠化帶來的影響，譬如採取（adopt）可持續的農耕模式，只是由於成本（cost）較高，許多農民難以負擔土地再生利用（reclamation）的費用。重新造林（reforestation）可以扭轉沙漠化，在雨季（rainy season）種下幼苗（seedling）有望徹底遏止沙漠化趨勢。

重要字彙	
desertification	沙漠化
bodies of water	水體
vegetation	植被
arid	乾旱
barren	貧瘠
immediate	直接的
deforestation	砍伐森林
overgrazing	過度放牧
sandstorm	沙塵暴
area	面積
ecological equilibrium	生態平衡

mitigate	減輕
reverse	逆轉
adopt	採取
cost	成本
reclamation	再生利用
reforestation	重新造林
rainy season	雨季
seedling	幼苗
延伸字彙	
biodiversity	物種多樣性
threat	威脅
endangered	瀕危的
shelter	遮蓋物
windbreaks	防風林
environmental volunteers	環保志工
rehabilitation	康復

Part 1

Part 2

Part 3

Part 4

Topic 42 清潔發展機制

　　清潔發展機制（Clean Development Mechanism/CDM）是一種減少溫室氣體排放（emissions reduction）的計畫。京都議定書（Kyoto Protocol）對已開發國家（developed country）有溫室氣體排放限量（emission limitation）規定，而這些國家通常不願降低能耗（energy consumption）以達到自己的減排承諾（commitment）。通過 CDM，已開發國家可以幫助開發中國家（developing country）發展減排項目，並購買這些項目中被認證的減排量（Certified Emissions Reduction/CER），以達到共贏（all-win）效果。與燃燒化石燃料（fossil fuel）發電不同，水電（hydropower）、風力發電（wind power）、生物質（biomass）發電、潮汐能（tidal power）、太陽能（solar power）等發電模式都可以避免排放溫室氣體。開發中國家建造清潔能源（clean energy）的發電項目可以藉由 CDM 獲得更多資金（funding）的支持。

重要字彙	
Clean Development Mechanism/CDM	清潔發展機制
emissions	排放
reduction	減少
Kyoto Protocol	京都議定書
developed country	已開發國家
emission limitation	排放限量
energy consumption	能耗
commitment	承諾
developing country	開發中國家

certified	被認證的
all-win	共贏
fossil fuel	化石燃料
hydropower	水電
wind power	風力發電
biomass	生物質
tidal power	潮汐能
solar power	太陽能
clean energy	清潔能源
funding	資金
延伸字彙	
framework	體系
flexible	可變通的
carbon trading	碳交易
executive	決策的
industrialise	工業化
additional	額外的
scheme	計畫

Part 2
答題技巧

Part 2
答題技巧

雅思聽力考試形式

聽力考試分為四個部分，每部分有 10 個題目。播放聽力內容是 30 分鐘，錄音只播放一次，在這段時間要閱讀問題並把答案寫在題目卷上。在聽力內容播放完畢後，有 10 分鐘的時間把答案謄寫到答題卡上和檢查答案。朗讀聽力內容的可能是各種口音的英文，如英國口音、美國口音、澳洲口音、印度口音等。

問題的排列順序和聽力內容中出現的順序一致。

雅思聽力四個部分的應答策略

雅思聽力考試的第 1、2 部分是社會生活類，內容是關於日常生活，如租房、旅行、看病、訂票等，測試聽力理解和紀錄事實性資訊的能力；3、4 部分是學術類，有學術演講、課堂討論、研討會、專題介紹等，測試對特定資訊、態度和觀點的理解。其中 1、3 部分通常為談話和討論，2、4 部分則為獨白。四個部分的難度是由易到難。

第 1 部分最容易，又和最難的第 4 部分一樣都出 10 題，因此要盡量在第一部分得到滿分。第 1 部分相對簡單會讓人放鬆警惕，反而會不小心錯過關鍵字。而第 1 部分倘若沒有答好，緊張的情緒會影響後面的測試，所以作答這部分試題應當集中精神。這部分的答案常會考到特定名詞的拼寫，需要注意的是有時朗讀者會先拼出一個錯誤單字再修改其中幾個字母；也要習慣一些對字母的描述，如 A for apple、G for great、double T 等。另外固有名詞的第一個字母要大寫，否則即使拼寫正確也不得分，如果習慣在答題卡上把所有單字都用 BLOCK LETTERS 拼寫，工整並且字母全部大寫，就可以預防這種情況的失分。答案是數字時不要忘記寫數字的單位，如 dollar、cm、km、am/pm、g 等。

第 2 部分是繼第 1 部分之後相對容易的單元，也須努力在這一部分取得滿分。就算答案沒有聽得很清楚或者剛好是不認識的單字，也應在聽到的當下馬上寫下來。如果因為不確定而留白，待到全部 section 念完再來作答，常會因為沒有做好標記而對答案全無印象。IELTS 考試的答題卡也一定不要留空白，即使選擇題之外的其他題目，用猜測作答猜中的概率極低，也應當把完全 miss 掉的題目填上一個合理推測的答案。

第 3、第 4 部分難度超過之前兩部分，前兩部分的應答策略是盡量減少不必要的失分項，拿到滿分；後兩部分的策略則是要把所有聽懂的部分全部答對。3、4 部分有比較大的機會會遇到一些瓶頸題目或是聽不懂的部分，這時就應暫時放棄被卡住的題目，專注作答後面的題目。因為所有題目都是按照聽力原文的順序給出，停在一道題目上思考影響後面題目的作答就得不償失。可以待到最後檢查和謄寫答案時，再來回答之前被暫時放棄的題目。如果是填空類題，在閱讀題目的時候，可以從語法層面和意義層面先設想出可能的答案，譬如根據問題推測答案是名詞、動詞或是形容詞、副詞，符合上下文意義的情況下有那些字彙可能出現，這樣可以在聽到錄音時更有效的捕捉到答案。

聽力錄音播放完畢後，有 10 分鐘時間將答案謄寫在答題卡上。

10 分鐘檢查答案並書寫整齊是剛好夠用，但是要寫的盡量快，如果花太多時間推敲答案就可能出現收卷時還沒有謄寫完畢的狀況。另外第一印象有可能最為準確，很多時候都有在謄寫時猶豫再三，把正確答案改成錯誤答案的情況。[1]

一些通用的技巧可以用於大多數題目中，如看清楚字數限制、畫出關鍵詞並預測答案、標註詞性、快速書寫、注意轉承連接詞、注意大小寫和單複數等。

雅思聽力考試的主要的題型

★ 填表／筆記／流程圖／總結題
★ 選擇題
★ 填空題
★ 完成句子
★ 為圖表、計畫或地圖做標記
★ 分類／配對題[2]

各種題型及解題技巧題型

以下部分選擇了 Cambridge IELTS 10、9、8、7 的聽力部分的一些題目，分別解析各種題型和解題技巧。

1. 填表／筆記／流程圖／總結題：

這種題型要求對聽力材料的內容／要點填空，題目一般是紀錄事實性資訊如名字、電話、地點、時間、價格等，或總結分類詳細的

---

1 ｵuIﾁｶ。でTOEICとIELTSのスコアを、Wげるı^ｻyｫjｱjɪk 。]http://thank.red/listening.html ^

2 British Council IELTS 考試準備指南 題型解析。

資訊，出現形式為表格、筆記、流程表、總結。

題目範例 1
Cambridge IELTS 10 Test 3 LISTENNING SECTION 1

Question 1-10

Complete the form below.

Write **ONE WORD AND/OR A NUMBER** for each answer.

Early Learning Childcare Centre
Enrolment Form
Example
Parent or guardian: Carol Smith
Personal Details
Child's name: Kate
Age: 1_____
Address: 2_____Road, Woodside, 4032
Phone: 33459865
Childcare Information
Day enrolled for: Monday and 3_____
Start time: 4_____ am
Childcare group: the 5_____group
Which meal/s are required each day? 6_____
Medical conditions: need 7_____
Emergency contact: Jenny 8_____Phone: 3346 7523
Relationship to child: 9_____
Fees
Will pay each 10_____

Q1 聽力原文：

DIRECTOR：Now, we have several groups at the center and we cater for children from three to five years old. How old is your daughter?

CAROL：She's three now but she turns four next month.

DIRECTOR：I'll put four down because that's how old she'll be when she starts.

解析

這一題問年齡，答案應該為一個數字。填表內容是幼稚園申請表，因而推測答案是幼稚園的入學年齡。How old is your daughter 是定位句子，據此判斷答案就在下一句的回答內容裡。回答先是 three，然後立刻修改為 four。這裏 three 是干擾項目，答案應當是 four。下一句也確認了 I'll put four down 因為四歲是她入學後的年齡。題目要求是一個字／數字，因而可以回答 4 或 four。

Q2 聽力原文:

DIRECTOR：That's good to hear. And what's your address?

CAROL：It's 46 Wombat Road, that's W-O-M-B-A-T. Woodside 4032.

解析

這一題要求回答地址，可以推測答案是路牌號加路名的組合。題目關鍵句 what's your address 被問出，下面的回答就是答案：46 Wombat。路名還被拼寫出來因此是相對容易的一問，要注意 W 大寫。

Q3 聽力原文：

DIRECTO：So, have you decided on the days you'd like to bring you daughter here?

CAROL：I'd prefer Monday and Wednesday if possible.

DIRECTOR：Mmm, I'll check, Monday is fine, but I think the center is already full for Wednesday. Erm. Yes. Sorry. It seems to be a very popular day. We can offer you a Thursday or a Friday as well.

CAROL：Oh dear, I suppose Thursday would be all right because she has swimming on Friday.

解析

題目問入學日期 Monday and_____，可以判斷出答案是 Tuesday 到 Friday 中的一天。首先已經聽到 I'd prefer Monday and Wednesday。聽力測試的慣例是太直接的答案之後會有修改，Director 表示 Wednesday 已經滿員，可以在 Thursday 和 Friday 中選一天。正確答案是 Thursday，答案句是 I suppose Thursday would be all right。

Q4 聽力原文：

DIRECTOR：Ok, got that. Because a lot of parents work, we do offer flexible start and finish times. We are open from 7:30 in the morning until 6 o'clock at night. What time would you like your daughter to start?

CAROL：I need to get to work in the city by 9:00 so I'll drop her off at 8:30. You are pretty close to the city here so that should give me plenty of time to get there.

解析

這題問上學時間，首先 Director 表示 7:30 之後的時間都可以開始，Carol 回答說她上班時間是 9:00，所以希望 8:30 送女兒上學。答案是 8:30。這一段裡面密集講出了幾個時間點，前面出現的幾個時間都是答案的條件。

Q5 聽力原文：

DIRECTOR：That's fine. Now, we also need to decide which group she'll be in. We have two different groups and they're divided up according to age. There's the green group, which is for three to four-year-old. And then there's the red group which is for four to five-year-old.

CAROL：She's quite mature for her age and she can already write her name and read a little.

DIRECTOR：Well, I'll put her in the red group and we can always change her to the green one if there are any problems.

解析

問題是要把小朋友分進哪個 group，這題沒有線索事先預測大概會填入什麼答案，需要在聽對話時候找到正確答案。Director 首先介紹 childcare center 的小朋友們被按照年齡分為 red、green 兩組，其中紅組年紀較大。Carol 回答她的女兒以年齡來看相對比較成熟，於是 Director 回答 I'll put her in the red group，答案是 red。

Q6 聽力原文：

DIRECTO：Ok. Let's move on to meals. We can provide breakfast, lunch and dinner. As she's finishing pretty early, she won't need dinner, will you give her breakfast before she comes?

CAROL：Yes, she'll only need lunch.

解析

問題是 which meals are required，推測答案是 breakfast，lunch 或 dinner。答案則直接回答了 she'll only need lunch。

Q7 聽力原文：

DIRECTOR：Now, does she have any medical conditions we need to know about? Dose she have asthma or any hearing problems for example?

CAROL：No. <u>But she dose need to wear glasses.</u>

解析

這一題要考 medical condition，答案應當為身體狀況相關的字彙。Director 詢問小孩子有沒有氣喘或聽力障礙，Carol 回答說沒有，但她需要戴眼鏡，所以答案為 glasses。

Q8/Q9 聽力原文：

DIRECTOR：Right. OK. Now, I also need emergency contact details.

CAROL：So what sort of information do you need?

DIRECTOR：Just the name and number of a friend or family member we can contact in case we can't get hold of you at any time.

CAROL：Ok. That'd better be my sister... Jenny <u>Ball</u>. That's B-A-double L. Her phone number is 3346 7523.

DIRECTOR：Great. So she is the child's <u>aunt</u>.

CAROL：That's right.

解析

第 8、9 兩問是接連出現的，都是有關緊急聯絡人的問題，問到對方的姓名和與小朋友的關係。這兩個問題分別都很容易答出，Ball 和 aunt 有在對話中清晰的出現。一個陷阱是之前的幾道題目給人的感覺是平均兩三組問答出一道題目，而這裏是連著出現的兩題。

Q10 聽力原文：

CAROL：What about payment? How much are the fees each term?

DIRECTOR：Well, for two days and the hours you've chosen, that will be $450 altogether.

CAROL：OK, and do I have to pay that now?

DIRECTOR：No, we send out invoices once the children start at the center. You can choose to pay at the end of each term or we do offer a slightly discounted rate if you <u>pay every month</u>.

CAROL：Oh, <u>I'll do that then</u>. I find it easier to budget that way and I'm not used to the term dates just yet.

解析

題目中這一題在 fee 的部分，所以聽到 What about payment?就標記題目的答案在接下來的對話裡。題目問 Will pay each_____，從 each 推測可能是要考付費的頻率而非價格。談話圍繞在一學期多少錢，然後 Director 提到如果按月付會有折扣。回答選擇了按月支付，所以答案應當是 month。

題目範例 2

Cambridge IELTS 9 Test 2 LISTENNING SECTION 2

Question 11-13

Complete the notes below.

Write **NO MORE THAN THREE WORDS** for each answer.

Parks and open spaces

Name of place	Of particular interest	Open
Halland Common	Source of River Ouse	24 hours
Holt Island	Many different 11_____	Between 12_____ and_____

	Reconstruction of a 2,000-yeat-old 13 ____ ____with activities for children	daylight hours
Longfield Country Park		

Q11/Q12 聽力原文：

Then there's Holt Island, which is noted for its great range of trees. In the past willows were grown here commercially for basket-making, and this ancient craft has recently been reintroduced. The island is only open to the public from Friday to Sunday, because It's quite small, and if there were people around every day, much of the wildlife would keep away.

解析

表格的標題 Parks and open spaces 表示文章會介紹下列的幾個公園和公共空間，三欄分別列出的是公園名稱、特點和開放時間。所以在聽錄音時可以著重注意對公園具體特徵的描述和有關時間的名詞。列表中第一個公園 Halland Common 沒有題目，錄音講到 Holt Island，標記了題目在下面的段落裡。Holt Island is noted for its great range of trees. Is noted for sth 是講此處的一個顯著特點，great range of 和題目中的 many different 是同義替換，關鍵字 trees 就是 Q11 的正確答案。

接下來補充說明了 Holt Island 的柳條曾被用來編籃子，現在也恢復了此一傳統。下一句說到了開放時間 is open to the public from Friday to Sunday，錄音中的 from... to... 對應題目中的 between... and...，所以 Q12 的答案是 Friday 和 Sunday。

Q13 聽力原文：

From there it's just a short walk across the bridge to Longfield

Country Park. <u>Longfiled has a modern replica of a farm from over two thousand years ago.</u>

解析

Longfield Country Park 標記這一題，題目中的 reconstruction of 和錄音中的 a modern replica 一致，因而答案是 farm。

題目範例 3

Cambridge IELTS 8 Test 4 LISTENNING SECTION 3

Question 27-30
Complete the flow-chart below.
Write **NO MORE THAN TWO WORDS AND/OR A NUMBER** for each answer.

Advice on exam preparation

Make sure you know the exam requirements

⇩

Find some past papers

⇩

Work out your 27_____for revision
and write them on a card

⇩

Make a 28_____ and keep it in view

⇩

Divide revision into 29_____for each day

⇩

Write one 30_____about each topic

⇩

Practise writing some exam answers

Q27 聽力原文：

JEANNIE：Well, the first thing is to find out exactly what's requited in the exams.

DAN：Mm. Would it help to get hold of some past papers?

JEANNIE：Yes. They'll help to make it clear.

DAN：Right, I'll do that. Then what?

JEANNIE：Then you can sort out your revision <u>priorities</u>, based on what's most likely to come up. I put these on a card, and read them through regularly.

解析

整個流程圖是關於如何複習備考的。全段對話一開始是兩人對大學生活各方面的討論，談到考試的部分則標記關於這部分題目的內容出現。前兩句有提到 find the exam requirements 和 find some past papers。題目問到 work out your_____for revision，對話裡對應的部分是 sort out your revisions priorities。Work out 與 sort out 表示一樣的意思 revisions priorities 則等同於 priorities for revision。答案是 priorities。

Q28 聽力原文：

JEANNIE：But that isn't enough in itself. You also need a <u>timetable</u>, to see how you can fit everything in, in the time available. Then keep it in front of you while you're studying.

解析

題目是 make a，可以推測答案是一個名詞。對話提到 need a timetable 雖然與 make a timetable 不完全相同，但從整個句子看 make a timetable and keep it in view 和 need a timetable and keep it in front of you 是同樣的意思。答案是 timetable。

Q29 聽力原文：

DAN：I've done that before, but it hasn't helped me!

JEANNIE：Maybe you need to do something different every day, so if you break down your revision into <u>small tasks</u>, and allocate them to specific days, there's more incentive to tackle them. With big topics you're more likely to out off starting.

解析

這一題承接上一題談到的做 timetable，Dan 認為做複習日程表沒有效用。Jeannie 解釋做計畫時應當把複習任務分散開來，每天做不一樣的事，break down your revision into small tasks，就是題目中的 divide revision into_____，此處答案就是 small tasks。題目要求 no more than two words，答為 small tasks 或 tasks 都可以。

Q30 聽力原文：

JEANNIE：And as I revise each topic I write a <u>single paragraph</u> about it – then later I can read it through quickly, and it helps fix things in my mind.

DAN：That's brilliant.

解析

題目是 write one_____about each topic，原文説 write a single paragraph about it，答案前後文字都和錄音中的一致，答案應當是 single paragraph。

題目範例 **4**

Cambridge IELTS 8 Test 2 LISTENNING SECTION 3

Question 25-30
Complete the summary below.
Write **ONE WORD ONLY** for each answer.

Looking for Asian honey bees Birds called Rainbow Bee Eaters eat only 25_____ , and cough up small bits of skeleton and other products in a pellet. Researchers go to the locations the bee eaters like to use for 26_____. They collect the pellets and take them to a 27_____ for analysis. Here 28_____ is used to soften them, and the researchers look for the 29_____ of Asian bees in the pellets. The benefit of this research is that the result is more 30_____ than searching for live Asian bees.

Q25 聽力原文：

PROFESSOR：How will you know if Asian bees have entered Australia?

GRANT：We're looking at the diet of the bird called the Rainbow Bee Eater. The Bee Eater <u>doesn't care what it eats, as long as they're insects.</u> But the interesting thing about this bird is that we are able to analyze exactly what it eats and that's really helpful if we're looking for introduced insects.

解析

Summary 的考題模式是將整個錄音內容整理成為相對簡練的段落，要求一邊聽錄音一邊總結歸納。因為題目的順序和聽力原文順序一致,且都有關鍵字做標記,所以難度與一般的填表題目相當。這部分題目之前的對話是講 Asian honey bees 如何對澳洲生態造成潛在威脅,涉及到 summary 題目的對話則圍繞如何找到 Asian honey bees。在錄音播放前就迅速瀏覽題目,得到 general ideas。

尋找 Asian honey bees 的辦法是借助叫做 Rainbow Bee Eaters 的鳥,Q25 問這種鳥唯一的食物是什麼,可以先依照常識推斷鳥類的食物會是穀類、植物或昆蟲,按照這一題的邏輯,也可能是蜜蜂。原文中標示答案的一句是 The Bee Eater doesn't care what it eats, as long as they're insects。只要是昆蟲就吃,因而答案是 insects。下一句也再次確認通過對這種鳥食物的分析來了解昆蟲。

Q26/Q27 聽力原文:

GRANT:Because insects have their skeletons outside their bodies, so the Bee Eaters digest the meat from the inside. Then they bring up all the indigestible bits of skeleton and, of course, the wings in a pellet – a small ball of waste material which they cough up.

PROFESSOR:That sounds a bit unpleasant. So, how do you go about it?

GRANT:In the field we track down the Bee Eaters and find their favorite <u>feeding</u> spots, you know, the places where the birds usually feed. It's here that we can find the pellet. We collect them up and take them back to the <u>laboratory</u> to examine the contents.

解析

題目中有一個多次出現的生詞 pellet,但不影響整段的理解,因為文中有具體解釋 a pellet – a small ball。Bee Eaters 會吐出 pellet,裡面裹著昆蟲沒有被消化的部分。作答 Q26 時,可以在問題紙上先畫出關鍵字 locations,以便聽到時馬上找到答案。原文說到 in the field 對應題目中的 the locations,地點就是這種鳥的 feeding spots，答案是 feeding。Q27 是把 pellet 帶去研究的地點，原文中 examine 對應 analysis，答案為 laboratory。

Q28/Q29 聽力原文：

PROFESSOR：How do you do that?

GRANT：The pellets are really hard, especially if they have been out in the sun for a few days so, fist of all, we treat them by adding water to moisten and make them softer. Then we pull them apart under the microscope. Everything's all scrunched up, but we're looking for wings so we just pull them all out and straighten them. Then we identify them to see if we can find any Asian bee wings.

解析

Q28 的關鍵字是 soften，鳥吐出很硬的小球，如果做分析要將其軟化。題目問加入什麼使得 pellet 變軟，原文講 we treat them by adding water to moisten and make them softer。答案為 water。

Q29 問研究者從 pellet 中尋找 Asian bees 的哪一部分，原文說 we identify them to see if we can find any Asian bee wings，所以 wings 是辨別出 Asian bees 的關鍵，答案為 wings。

Q30 聽力原文：

PROFESSOR：And how many have you found?

GRANT：So far our research shows that Asian bees have not entered Australia in any number – it's a good result and much more reliable than trying to find live ones as evidence of introduced insects.

解析

題目要求回答這種研究方法比其他尋找 Asian bees 的辦法更如何，所以用 the result is more 來定位，答案是 reliable。

2. 選擇題

選擇題的出題形式可能是一個問題，或一個句子的前半段，要從 A、B、C 三個選項中選出正確／最佳答案；或者是從多種選項中選出二或三個正確答案。選擇題要求對段落大意和細節都有足夠理解。應當盡量在聽力播放之前把所有選擇題的題目和選項讀完，並畫出關鍵字。

題目範例 1

Cambridge IELTS 10 Test 2 LISTENNING SECTION 2

Question 11-20

Choose the correct letter, **A, B** *or* **C.**

New city developments

⑪ The idea for the two new developments in the city came from
   A local people
   B the City Council
   C the SWRDC

⑫ What is unusual about Brackenside pool?
   A its architectural style
   B its heating system
   C its method of water treatment

⑬ Local newspapers have raise worries about
   A the late opening date.
   B the cost of the project.
   C the size of the facilities.

⑭ What decision has not yet been made about the pool?
   A whose status will be at the door
   B the exact opening times
   C who will open it

Q11 聽力原文：

Good morning, I'm very pleased to have this opportunity to say a little about two exciting new developments in the city: the Brackenside Open-Air Swimming Pool and the children's Adventure Playground in Central Park. As many of you may know, the idea for these initiatives came from you, the public. In the extensive consultation exercise which the City Council conducted last year. And they have bee realized using money the SWRDC – the South West Regional Development Commission.

解析

Q11 問的是城市的兩項新建設項目的創意來自哪裏，選項分別是 local people，the City Council 和 the SWRDC。在聽力播放時按照關鍵字 idea 定位，聽到 the idea for these initiatives came from you, the public。確定答案 A。The City Council 和 the SWRDC 也分別在後面的句子出現，一個是項目實施者，另一個是投資方。需要清楚聽懂選項中的這三種人物／機構的角色，才不會被干擾項目影響。

Q12 聽力原文：

First of all, Brackenside Pool. As many of the older members of the audience will remember, there used to be a wonderful open-air pool on the sea front 30 years ago but it had to close when it was judged to be unsafe. For the design of this new heated pool, we were very happy to secure the talents of internationally renowned architect Ellen Wendon, who has managed to combine a charming 1930s design, which fits in so well many of the other buildings in the area, with up-to-the-minute features such as a recycling system – the only one of its kind in the world – which enables seawater to be used in the pool.

解析

Q12 提問 Brackenside Pool 有什麼與眾不同之處，可選擇的項目有它的建築風格、供熱系統和水處理方法。原文敘述 Pool 融合了 1930 年代的風格和時下最先進的技術，技術的舉例就是 a recycling system，可以使海水得到運用。recycling system 是一種 method of water treatment，答案和原文用了同義替換的方式，並沒有相同的單字出現，所以要透過理解得出結論。B 選項的 heating system 有 system 一字，是使人容易受到誤導的干擾選項。正確答案為 C。

Q13 聽力原文：

Now, there has been quite a bit of discussion in the local press about whether there would be enough room for the number of visitors we're hoping to attract, but the design is deceptive and there have been rigorous checks about capacity. Also, just in case you were wondering, we're on schedule for a June 15th opening date and well within budget: a testimony to the excellent work of local contracts Hickman's.

解析

題目是當地報紙對游泳池項目有何種憂慮，閱讀題目時先畫出選項中的關鍵字 date、cost、size。這一題的關鍵句緊接著上一題，所以聽錄音時須保持精神集中，因為題目有時會密集出現。Quite a bit of discussion in the local press 等同於 local newspapers have raised worries about，後面句子應當就是正確答案，whether there would be enough room 談到的是 size 的問題，因而選擇 C。後句的 capacity 也對答案再次確認。

Q14 聽力原文：

We hope that as many people as possible will be there on June 15th. We have engaged award-winning actress Coral White to declare the pool open and there'll be drinks and snacks available the pool side. <u>There'll also be a competition for public to decide on the sculpture we plan to have at the entrance</u>; you will decide which famous historical figure from the city we should have.

解析

Q14 要選擇的是還有哪一件事未完成，選項有門前雕像的選擇、開幕時間和誰來為泳池揭幕。聽力原文中提到了游泳池正式對公眾開放的時間是 June 15th，由著名女星主持開幕。唯一沒有定案的項目是入口處要擺放誰的 sculpture，由大眾票選這個城市的著名歷史人物。答案是 A。

題目範例 2

Cambridge IELTS 10 Test 2 LISTENNING SECTION 3

Question 21 and 22
*Choose **TWO** letters, **A–E**.*
Which **TWO** hobbies was Thor Heyerdahl very interested in as a youth?

   A camping
   B climbing
   C collecting
   D hunting
   E reading

Question 23 and 24
*Choose **TWO** letters, **A–E**.*
Which do the speakers say are the **TWO** reasons why Heyerdahl went to live on an island?

   A to examine ancient carvings

Part 1
Part 2
Part 3
Part 4

B to experience an isolated place

C to formulate a new theory

D to learn survival skills

E to study the impact of an extreme environment

Q21/Q22 聽力原文：

VICTOR：Right, well, for our presentation shall I start with the early life of Thor Heyerdahl?

OLIVIA:：Sure. Why don't you begin with describing the type of boy he was, <u>especially his passion for collecting things</u>.

VICTOR：That's right, he had his own little museum. And I think it's unusual for children to develop their own values and not join in their parents' hobbies; I'm thinking of how Heyerdahl wouldn't go hunting with his dad, for example.

OLIVIA:：Yeah, he preferred to learn about nature by listening to his mother read to him. And quite early on he knew he wanted to become an explorer when he grew up. That came from his camping trips he went on in Norway I think...

VICTOR：<u>No, it was climbing that he spent his time on as a young man.</u>

解析

題目要求選擇 Heyerdahl 青年時代的的兩項愛好，聽力原文中首先談到 his passion for collecting things，he had his own little museum，所以 collecting 是答案之一。對話又說 Heyerdahl 沒有被父母的興趣所影響，he wouldn't go hunting with his dad，因此 hunting 被排除掉。接下來 Olivia 提到 Heyerdahl 小時候喜歡透過聽母親講故事認識自然，並推測是挪威之旅使得他很早就決定做探險家，這一句涉及到 reading 和 camping 兩個干擾選項。然後假設被下一句否定：No, it was climbing that he spent his time on as a young man，表明 Heyerdahl 的另一項愛好是 climbing。答案是 B 和 C。

Q23/Q24 聽力原文：

OLIVIA：：Oh, right... After university he married a classmate and together, they decided <u>to experience living on a small island</u>, <u>to find out how harsh weather conditions shaped people's lifestyles.</u>

解析

這兩題要回答的是 Heyerdahl 去島上生活的原因，原文中的 to experience living on a small island 對應答案中的 to experience an isolated place；原文中的 to find out how harsh weather conditions shaped people's lifestyles 對應答案中的 to study the impact of an extreme environment。答案為 B 和 E。原文也提到 Heyerdahl 學習了島上生存技巧，又受到古典雕刻的啟發，構建了新的理論，但這幾個選項都不是去島上生活的 reasons。

題目範例 3

Cambridge IELTS 9 Test 4 LISTENNING SECTION 4

Question 31-36
*Choose the correct letter, **A, B** or **C**.*

Wildlife in city gardens

㉛ What lead the group to choose their topic?
　　A They were concerned about the decline of one species.
　　B They were interested in the effect of city growth.
　　C They wanted to investigate a recent phenomenon.

㉜ The exact proportion of land devoted to private gardens was confirmed by

A consulting some official documents.

B taking large-scale photos.

C discussions with town surveyors.

㉝ The group asked garden owners to

A take part in formal interviews.

B keep a record of animals they saw.

C get in contact when they saw a rare species.

㉞ The group made their observations in gardens

A which had a large number of animal species.

B which they considered to be representative.

C which had stable populations of rare animals.

㉟ The group did extensive reading on

A wildlife problems in rural areas.

B urban animal populations.

C current gardening practices.

㊱ The speaker focuses on three animal species because

A a lot of data has been obtained about them.

B the group were most interested in them.

C they best indicated general trends.

Q31 聽力原文：

First of all, how did we choose our topic? Well. There are four of us in the group and one day while we were discussing a possible focus, <u>two of the group mentioned that they had seen yet more sparrow-hawks - one of Britain's most interesting birds of prey – in their own city center gardens and wondered why they were turning up in these gardens in great numbers.</u> We were all very engaged by the idea of why wild animals would choose to inhabit a city garden

解析

這是一篇 wildlife project presentation，出現在 Section 4 有一定難度，在錄音播放前的題目閱讀量比較大，需要很快的跳讀所有問題和答案，並標記關鍵字。Q31 要解答的是這一組同學選擇題材的原因，選項標記的關鍵字分別是 species decline、city growth effect 和 investigate phenomenon。聽力原文說到兩名小組成員發現很多數量的 sparrow-hawks 出現在 city center gardens，他們好奇為什麼會有這種情況發生，因而答案為 C。sparrow-hawks 沒有數量減少的問題，也不是城市化導致的結果，由此排除 A、B。

Q32 聽力原文：

The first thing we did was to establish what proportion of the urban land is taken up by private gardens. We estimated that it was about one fifth, and <u>this was endorsed by looking a large-scale usage maps in the town land survey office</u> – 24% to be precise.

解析

這一題考點相對直接，問如何確認了私人花園用地佔整個城市的比率。Endorsed by 和問題中的 confirmed by 都表示被認可、確認，原文答案是運用了 a large-scale usage maps in the town land survey office，土地調研辦公室的大範圍地圖，並非 B 選項提到的 photos，也不是 C 選項與測繪者討論得來。Town land survey office 證明是 official documents。正確答案為 A。

Q33 聽力原文：

Our own informal discussions with neighbors and friends led us to believe that many garden owners had interesting experiences to relate regarding wild animal sightings so we decided<u> to survey</u>

garden owners from different areas of the city. Just over 100 of them completed a survey once every two weeks for twelve month – ticking off species they had seen from a pro forma list – and adding the names of any rarer ones.

解析

題目問研究小組讓 garden owners 做了什麼，三個選項分別是現場採訪、紀錄看見的動物、以及看到罕見生物就聯繫小組成員。聽力原文說是一個持續一年，每隔兩週做一次的 survey，因而排除 A （interview）。而整個 survey 是在 list 上面做紀錄，所以排除 C （get in contact）。正確答案為 B。

Q34 聽力原文：

Meanwhile, we were doing our own observations in selected gardens throughout the city. We deliberately chose smaller ones because they were by far the most typical in the city. The whole point of the project was to look at the norm not the exception.

解析

這一題要考的是小組選擇了怎樣的公園來觀察，we were doing our own observations 標記這之後的句子就是他們的選擇原則：the most typical，之後有進一步說明他們要觀察通例而非特例。A 選項動物種類多的，B 選項有代表性的，C 選項動物數量穩定的。只有 B 符合小組選擇標準，為正確答案。

Q35 聽力原文：

Alongside this primary research on urban gardens, we were studying a lot of books about the decline of wild animals in the countryside and think of possible causes for this.

解析

提問研究小組對什麼內容做了廣泛閱讀，原文中 we were studying a lot of books 對應題目中的 extensive reading，study 的內容是 about the decline of wild animals in the countryside，尋找鄉下野生動物減少的原因。正確答案為 A，wildlife problems in rural areas。B 城市動物數量與 C 園藝操作是無關的選項。

Q36 聽力原文：

What we've decided to present today is information about just three species – because we felt these gave a good indication of the processes at work in rural and urban settings as a whole.

解析

題目問演講者會著重談到三種動物的原因是什麼，原文的解釋是這三種動物是 a good indication of the processes at work in rural and urban settings as a whole，等同與 C 選項的 indicate general trend。正確答案為 C。A 資料充足與 B 符合小組的興趣並未被提及。

題目範例 4

Cambridge IELTS 8 Test 1 LISTENNING SECTION 2

Question 16-18
*Choose **THREE** letters, **A-G**.*
Which **THREE** things can students have with them in the museum?

A food
B water
C cameras
D books
E bags

F pens

G worksheets

聽力原文：

When the students come into the museum foyer we ask them to check in their backpacks with their books, lunch boxes, etc, at the cloakroom before they enter the museum proper. I'm afraid in the past we have had a few things gone missing after school visits so this is a strict rule. Also, some of the exhibits are fragile and we don't want them to be accidentally knocked. But we do provide school students with handouts with questions and quizzes on them. There's so much that students can learn in the museum and it's fun for them to have something to do. Of course they'll need to bring something to write with for these. We do allow students to take photographs. For students who are doing projects it's useful to make some kind of visual record of what they see that they can add to their reports. And finally, they should not bring anything to eat into the museum, or drinks of any kind.

解析

題目要求從 7 個選項中選出三項學生可以帶進博物館的物品。原文先說進入博物館前廳時就要寄存背包、書和午餐，所以排除 A、D、E。解題關鍵句 But we do provide school students with handouts with questions and quizzes on them，博物館會為學生提供講義，上面有問題可以作答。Handouts with questions 和答案中的 worksheets 為同義替換，確定 G 為正確答案。另一個包含答案的句子是 they'll need to bring something to write with for these，表示 F 選項 pens 是另一個答案。We do allow students to take photographs 允許學生拍照則側面說明 cameras 也可以帶入展廳。這一段落的最末句說 they should not bring anything to eat into the museum, or drinks of any kind，不能攜帶任何食品和飲料，則 B 選項 water 也被排除。這一題的答案是 C、F、G。

題目範例 5

Cambridge IELTS 8 Test 1 LISTENNING SECTION 3

Question 25-27
*Choose **THREE** letters, **A-G**.*
Which **THREE** topics does Sandra agree to include in the proposal?

A climato changc
B ficld trip activitics
C geographical features
D impact of tourism
E myth and legends
F plant and animal life
G social history

聽力原文：
TUTOR：Interesting. Right, let's look at the content of your proposal now.
SANDRA：Did you find it comprehensive enough?
TUTIR：Well, yes and no. You've listed several different topics on your contents page, but I'm not sure they're all relevant.
SANDRA：No? Well, I thought that from the perspective of a field trip, one thing I needed <u>to focus on was the sandstone plateau and cliffs themselves</u>. The way they tower up from the flat landscape is just amazing. The fact that the surrounding softer rocks were eroded by wind and rain, leaving these huge outcrops high above the plain. It's hardly surprising that tourists flock to see the area.

TUTOR：Well, yes, I'd agree with including those points...

SANDRA：And then the fact that it's been home to native American Navajos and all the social history that goes with that. The hardships they endured trying to save their territory from the invading settlers. Their culture is so rich – all those wonderful stories.

TUTOR：Well, I agree it's interesting, but it's not immediately relevant to your proposal, Sandra, so at this stage, I suggest you focus on other considerations. I think an indication of what the students on the trip could actually do when they get there should be far more central, so that certainly needs to be included and to be expanded upon. And I'd like to see something about the local wildlife, and vegetation too, not that I imagine there's much to see. Presumably the tourist invasion hasn't helped.

SANDRA：Okay, I'll do some work on those two areas as well. But you're right, there's not much apart from some very shallow-rooted species. Although it's cold and snowy there in the winter, the earth is baked so hard in the summer sun that rainwater can't penetrate. So it's a case of flood or drought, really.

解析

題目問的是 Sandra 同意在她的研究計畫中加入哪些主題（課題科目是 Geographical Society field trip competition），第一個關鍵句是 one thing I needed to focus on was the sandstone plateau and cliffs themselves. 重點之一是砂岩高原和峭壁本身。對應 C 選項，geographical features。Sandra 又認為 social history of the native American Navajos 也很有意義，但 Tutor 否定了這個觀點，因為它雖然有趣但和主題並不直接相關，所以排除了 G 選項。Tutor 建議説 what the students on the trip could actually do when they get there 更為重要，也希望能夠看到 something about the local wildlife, and vegetation。這兩個建議被 Sandra 接納，I'll do some work on those two areas。所以 B field trip activities 和 F plant and animal life 是 Tutor 的兩個建議也應作為正確選項。Tourism impact 被認為對當地動植物沒有影響；climate change 和 legends 則沒有提及。答案為 B、C、F。

3. 填空題

　　前述的第一種題型：完成填表、記筆記、流程圖、總結類也是填空題的一種，除了以上幾種形式外，填空題也有分類比較型、圖形標籤型、簡答型等各種樣式。回答填空題是要求閱讀完題目後，用聽力入容中的資訊回答問題或列舉內容，答案通常被限定為不超過三個單字和/或一個數字。需要注意的是縮寫的單字不會被作為答案，帶有連字元的單字則算一個字。

題目範例 1

Cambridge IELTS 9 Test 4 LISTENNING SECTION 3

Question 26-30
Answer the questions below.
Write **NO MORE THAN THREE WORDS AND/OR A NUMBER** for each answer.

㉖ How did students do their practical sessions?

㉗ In the second semester how often did Kira work in a hospital?__ _____

㉘ How much full-time work did Kira do during the year?_____

㉙ Having completed the year, how does Kira feel?_____

㉚ In addition to the language, what did overseas students need to become familiar with?_____

Q26 – Q28 聽力原文：

PAUL：And how is your timetable? Was it a very busy year?

KIRA：Very, very busy. They make you work very hard. Apart from lectures, we had practical sessions in a lot of subjects. <u>We did these in small groups</u>. I had to go and work for four hours every week in a community pharmacy. Actually, I enjoyed this very much – meeting new people all the time. Then in second semester, we had to get experience in hospital dispensaries, so <u>every second day we went to one of the big hospitals and worked there</u>. And on top of all that we had our assignments, which took me a lot of time. Oh, I nearly forgot, between first and second semesters, <u>we had to work full-time for two weeks in a hospital</u>.

解析

Q26 問的是學生的實習是怎樣的狀況，原文說 we had practical sessions in a lot of subjects，we did these in small groups。就回答了 How 的問題，因而可以用聽力原文中的話來回答：groups 或 in small groups。Q27 問在第二學期，kira 多久去醫院工作一次，原文中 then in second semester 是標記的句子，後面有回答 every second day／every 2 days 是在醫院做事的頻率。Q28 的關鍵字是 full-time work，答案為 two weeks／2 weeks。這幾題可以直接寫下來對話裡面提到的正確答案或意義相同的說法，在聽力錄音播放前就畫出問題的關鍵字，聽到答案時則要快速寫下來。

Q29 聽力原文：

PAUL：That does sound a very heavy year. So are you pleased now that you did it? Do you feel some sense of achievement?

KIRA：Yeah, <u>I do feel much more confident</u>, which I suppose is the most important thing.

128

解析

Q29 問到完成這一年後 Kira 的感覺如何，答案為 confident。題目要求答案不超過三個字，因此答為 more confident 或 much more confident 也正確。

Q30 聽力原文：

PAUL：Anything else?

KIRA：Well, as I said before, <u>the biggest problem for me was a lack if familiarity with the education system here.</u>

解析

Q30 要回答除了外語，海外學生還應該熟悉什麼，用 Kira 的原話回答就是 education system。

題目範例 2

Cambridge IELTS 7 Test 3 LISTENNING SECTION 4

Question 35-40

Complete the notes below.

Write **ONE WORD ONLY** for each answer.

A company providing luxury serviced apartment aims to:

cater specifically for 35_____travellers

provide a stylish 36_____for guests to use

set a trend throughout the 37_____which becomes permanent

Traditional holiday hotels attract people by:

offering the chance to 38_____their ordinary routine life

making sure that they are cared for in all respect – like a 39_____

leaving small treats in their rooms – e.g. cosmetics or 40_____

Q35 – Q37 聽力原文：

However, nothing stands still in this world. One company has come up with the slogan 'Take Your Home With You', and aims to provide clients with luxury serviced apartment. Those in the business travel industry maintain that these serviced apartments dispense with all the unwanted and expensive hotel services that business travellers don't want, while maximizing the facilities they do want. For example, not only sleeping and living accommodation, but also a sleek modern kitchen that allows guests to cook and entertain if they wish, at no additional cost. The attractions of such facilities are obvious and it'll be interesting to see whether the company manages to establish a trend all over the world and make a lasting impact on the luxury accommodation market.

解析

這三題要回答奢華公寓是為了滿足哪一種旅行者的需求，提供時髦的什麼物品給客人使用，以及在什麼地方造就永久的時尚風格。聽力原文中提到這種公寓是相對 business travel industry 中昂貴又不實用的服務型公寓而言，去掉了不受歡迎的項目，增加了客戶需要的設施，服務的受眾則是 business travellers。Q35 答案為 business。對這種新型公寓的特點，舉例是它提供 a sleek modern kitchen，sleek 與題目中的 stylish 都是流行的、時髦的意思，因此 Q36 答案是 kitchen。新公寓的優勢非常明顯，就看公司是否有辦法使之成為 a trend all over the world，Q37 答案為 world。

Q38 – Q40 聽力原文：

Now, finally I want to consider the psychology underpinning the traditional holiday hotel industry. As a hotelier, how do you go about attracting people to give up the security of their own home and entrust themselves to staying in a completely strange place and sleeping in an unfamiliar bed? Firstly, hotels exploit people's <u>need to escape</u> the predictabilities and can indulge themselves. Secondly, there is something very powerful in our need to be pampered and looked after, it's almost <u>as if we return to being a baby</u>, when everything was done for us and we felt safe and secure, And not far removed from this is the pleasure in being spoilt and given little treats – like miniscule bottles of shampoo and tiny bars of soap, <u>the chocolate</u> on our pillow at night - and we actually forgot that we are paying for it all!

解析

問題為傳統的度假飯店用什麼來吸引客人，原文敘述著以旅館老闆身分來分析其中的原因。Firstly 是住外面令人從可預測的生活中逃離出來得到放鬆 the predictabilities 對應問題句裡的 ordinary routine life，Q38 答案為 escape。Secondly 是人的一種被照顧被縱容的心理，就像回到小嬰兒時期，什麼都不用做而感受到安全，原文裡 need to be pampered and looked after 和問題句中 are cared for in all respect 相同，舉例是 baby，為 Q39 的答案。另一個原因則是人們希望得到小禮物，舉例有 shampoo、soap、chocolate，前兩項都是 cosmetics，Q40 答案是 chocolate。

Cambridge IELTS 10 Test 4 LISTENNING SECTION 4

Question 34-40
Complete the notes below.
Write **ONE WORD ONLY** for each answer.

Uses of Nanotechnology

Transport

Nanotechnology could allow the development of stronger 34_____

Planes would be much lighter in weight.

35_____ travel will be made available to the masses.

Technology

Computers will be even smaller, faster, and will have a greater 36____

____

37_____ energy will become more affordable.

The Environment

Nano-robots could rebuild the ozone layer.

Pollutions such as 38_____ could be removed from water more easily.

There will be no 39_____ from manufacturing.

Health and Medicine

New methods of food production could eradicate famine.

Analysis of medical 40_____ will be speeded up.

Life expectancy could be increased.

Q34／Q35 聽力原文：

Thanks to nanotechnology, there could be a major breakthrough in the field of transportation with <u>the production of more durable</u>

metals. These could be virtually unbreakable, lighter and much more liable leading to planes that are 50 times lighter than at present. Those same improved capabilities will <u>dramatically reduce the cost of travelling into space</u> making it more accessible to ordinary people and opening up to a totally new holiday destination.

解析

這兩題考的是奈米技術應用交通領域，需要注意的重點字是 stronger …和…travel。原文說到 the production of more durable metals，durable 和 stronger 都有更堅硬耐用的意思，可以判斷 Q34 的答案為 metals。奈米技術還可以 reduce the cost of travelling into space，表示 Q35 答案為 space。

Q36／Q37 聽力原文：

In terms of technology, the computer industry will be able to shrink computer parts down to minute sizes. We need nanotechnology in order to create <u>a new generation of computers that will work even faster and will have a million times more memory but will be about the size of a sugar cube.</u> Nanotechnology could also revolutionise the way we generate power. <u>The cost of solar cells will be drastically reduced so harnessing this energy will be far more economical than at present.</u>

解析

在技術面的應用，Q36 題目是電腦會變得更小、更快並且有 greater…，原文提到新一代的電腦 will work even faster，will have a million times more memory 和 will be about the size of a sugar cube。所以答案應當是 memory。Q37 問哪一種能源會變的更便宜，原文說 the cost of solar cells will be drastically reduced，可以得知降價的應當是太陽能，答案為 solar。

Q38／Q39 聽力原文：

But nanotechnology has much wider applications than this and could have an enormous impact on our environment. For instance, ting airborne nano-robots could be programmed to actually rebuild the ozone layer, which could lessen the impact of global warming on our planet. That's pretty amazing thought, isn't it? On a more local scale, this new technology could help with the clean-up of environment disasters as nanotechnology will allow us to remove oil and other contaminations from the water far more effectively. And, if nanotechnology progresses as expected - as a sort of building block set of about 90 atoms - then you could build anything you wanted from the bottom up. In terms of production, this means that you only use what you need and so there wouldn't be any waste.

解析

這兩題考察奈米技術應用於環境，從題目可以看到主要有三方面的應用：修復臭氧層空洞的機器人、污水淨化（要考污染物的名稱）和製造業某種物質的零排放。原文講 nanotechnology will allow us to remove oil and other contaminations from the water，可以移除油和其他污染物，Q38 答案為 oil。Q39 對應原文中的 there wouldn't be any waste，答案為 waste。

Q40 聽力原文：

But it's in the area of medicine that nanotechnology may have its biggest impact How we detect disease will change as tiny biosensors are developed to analyse tests in minutes rather than days. There's even speculation nano-robots that could be used to slow the aging process, lengthening life expectancy.

解析

醫學、健康方面應用的考點是奈米技術會加速 analysis of medical ... 聽力原文中的關鍵字 analyse 出現，後面的單字 tests 就是 Q40 的答案。

4. 完成句子

這種題目類型要求先閱讀一組句子，這些句子一般情況下不是聽力原文中的原句，而是對聽力內容的一部分或是全部內容的總結，需要實用聽力內容中的資訊來回答句子裡挖空的部分。答案所用的單字都是直接從聽力原文中聽到的單字。回答這種題目要遵守字數限制並留意大小寫。

題目範例 1

Cambridge IELTS 9 Test 4 LISTENNING SECTION 3

Question 23-25
Complete the sentences below.
Write **ONE WORD ONLY** for each answer.

㉓ Kira says that lecturers are easier to_____ than those in her home country.

㉔ Paul suggests that Kira may be more_____ than when she was studying before.

㉕ Kira says that students want to discuss things that worry them or that_____them very much.

Q23-Q25 聽力原文：

PAUL：And what about the lectures themselves? Are they essentially the same as lecturers in your country?

KIRA：Well actually, no. Here, they're much easier to approach.

After every lecture you can go and ask them something you didn't understand. Or you can make an appointment and talk to them about anything in the course.

PAUL：Maybe you found them different because <u>you're a mature student now</u>, whereas when you were studying in your country you were younger and not so assertive.

KIRA：No, I don't think that's the difference. Most of the students here do it. In my faculty, they all seem to make appointments – usually to talk about something in the course that's worrying them. But <u>sometimes just about something that might really interest them,</u> something they might want to specialize in. The lectures must set aside certain times every week when they're available for students.

PAUL：That's good to hear.

解析

Q23Kira 說這裏的老師比她原本國家的老師 easier to⋯，原文中有相似的説法 Here, they're much easier to approach. 答案為 approach。Q24 Paul 覺得 Kira 比她之前 more⋯，原文中 Paul 説 you're a mature student now, when you were studying in your country you were younger。所以答案是 mature。Q25Kira 説學生們會討論 worry them 和⋯ them 的事，原文中對應的句子是 sometimes just about something that might really interest them，因而答案為 interest。

題目範例 2

Cambridge IELTS 8 Test 1 LISTENNING SECTION 3

Question 28-30

Complete the sentences below.

Write **ONE WORD AND/OR A NUMBER** for each answer.

㉘ The tribal park covers_____hectares.

㉙ Sandra suggested that they share the_____for transport.

㉚ She says they could also explore the local_____.

Q28-Q30 聽力原文：

TUTOR：So, you mentioned the monoliths and the spires, which was good, but what area does the tribal park cover? Do you know?

SANDRA：<u>12,000</u> hectares, and the plain is at about 5,850 meters above sea level.

TUTOR：Larger than I expected. Okay. Where's the nearest accommodation? That's a practical detail that you haven't included. Have you done any research on that?

SANDRA：Yes. There's nowhere to stay in the park itself, but there's an old trading post called Goulding quite near. All kinds of tours start from Goulding, too.

TUTOR：What kind of tours?

SANDRA：Well, the most popular are in four-wheel drive jeeps — but I wouldn't recommend hiring those. I think the best way to appreciate the area would be to hire <u>horses</u> instead and trek around on those. Biking is not allowed and it's impossible to drive around the area in private vehicles. The tracks are too rough.

TUTOR：Okay, lastly, what else is worth visiting there?

SANDRA：There are several <u>caves</u>, but I haven't looked into any details. I'll find out about them.

解析

Q28 問題是 tribal park 的面積，Sandra 回答有 12,000 hectares，因此答案是 12,000。Q29 是推薦的交通工具問題，four-wheel drive jeeps 是目前最流行的，但 Sandra 推薦的是租馬來騎，所以答案為 horses。Q30 問還可以探訪當地的什麼，這一問題的標記句是 Tutor 的問題 what else is worth visiting there，Sandra 回答 there are several caves，但她還沒有仔細關注過，由此判斷答案應當是 caves。

題目範例 3

Cambridge IELTS 7 Test 1 LISTENNING SECTION 3

Question 28-30

Complete the sentences below.

Write **ONE WORD ONLY** for each answer.

㉘ All managers need to understand their employees and recognize their company's_____ .

㉙ When managing change, increasing the company's_____ may be more important than employee satisfaction.

㉚ During periods of change, managers may have to cope with increased amounts of_____.

Q28-Q30 聽力原文：

TUTOR：To come back to you, Philip. You were saying that recognition of good performance is essential. What else should managers be looking for?

PHILIP：Well, managing people means you not only have an understanding of your employees, but you also <u>recognize the culture</u> of the organisation. In fact, for some organisations creativity and individuality may be the last thing they want to see during working hours!

TUTOR：Very true.

PHILIP：Yes, but managing people isn't as easy as it looks. For example, change in the workplace can be quite tricky, especially if there's a need to increase profit. And at times like these managers may have to give priority to profit rather individual staff needs.

TUTOR：Yes, and that creates difficult situations for people.

PHILIP：Yes but what's important is that managers are able to deal with quite high levels of personal stress. During times of change they should be thinking not only about the strain on their staff but take time out to think of themselves.

解析

Q28 要完成的句子是所有的管理者應當理解他們的僱員並 recognise their company's…，聽力原文中 managing people means you not only have an understanding of your employees, but you also recognise the culture of the organization. 關鍵字 recognise 後面的名詞就是答案 culture。Q29 需要完成的句子是當管理模式改變時，increase the company's… 也許比員工滿意度更為重要，作答這一題對應的原文中句子是 managers may have to give priority to profit rather individual staff needs. 優先權給予 profit(s)，是這一題的答案。Q30 問題為在改變發生時，管理層需要應對 increased amount of…，原文中的 during times of change 和原文 during periods of change 相同，後接 they should be thinking not only about the strain on their staff but take time out to think of themselves,員工和管理者自己身上增加的壓力，答案為原文中的 strain，或相同意義的 stress。

題目範例 **4**

Cambridge IELTS 7 Test 1 LISTENNING SECTION 4

Question 36-40
Complete the sentences below.
Write **ONE WORD ONLY** for each answer.

㊱ If you look at a site from a_____, you reduce visitor pressure.

㊲ To camp on a site may be disrespectful to people from that____
____.

㊳ Undiscovered material may be damaged by_____ .

㊴ You should avoid_____or tracing rock art as it is so fragile.

㊵ In general, your aim is to leave the site_____.

Q36 聽力原文：

Whenever you do go to a site, don't forget you can learn many things from <u>observing at a distance</u> instead of walking all over it. This can really help to reduce visitor pressure. People often say, 'Well, there's only two of us and just this one time', but maybe thousands of people are saying the same thing.

解析
原文中 observing at a distance can really help to reduce visitor pressure 符合問題 look at a site from... you reduce visitor pressure。應當填 distance。

Q37/Q38 聽力原文：

And then some basic rules to guide you – we'll have our own camp near a village, but remember never to camp on a site if you go on your own. It may be disrespectful to the <u>people of that culture</u>, and certainly <u>don't make fires</u>, however romantic it may seem. It's really

dangerous in dry areas, and you <u>can easily burn priceless</u>
<u>undiscovered material by doing so.</u>

解析

Q37 露營可能對哪些人不尊重，答案為 culture，people from/of that
culture。Q38 未被發掘的珍貴物質會被什麼東西毀壞，原文說 you
can easily burn priceless undiscovered material by doing so。這裏
的 so 指的是前文的 make fires，因而答案為 fire（s）。

Q39 聽力原文：

So, how are we going to enjoy the rock art on our field trip? By
looking at it, drawing it and photographing it – <u>NEVER by touching</u> it
or even tracing it. Rock art is fragile and precious.

解析

由於岩石非常脆弱，應當避免... or tracing it。Tracing 此處的意思是
將紙張拓在石頭上摹圖，原文中 touching 和 tracing 連在一起講，答
案 touching。

Q40 聽力原文：

And lastly please don't even move rocks or branches to take
photographs – <u>you should leave the site intact</u> – I'm sure I can rely
on you to do that.

解析

遊客應當 leave the site intact，答案為 intact。

5. 為圖表、計畫或地圖做標記

　　這類題目是在畫圖（例如某種設備）、圖片、平面圖、地圖等
圖形上完成標記工作，問題常會提供一組備選答案，要求把答案對應
的字母填在正確的位置上。也有可能是填空題。

題目範例 1

Cambridge IELTS 9 Test 4 LISTENNING SECTION 2

Question 11-13

Label the diagram below.

Choose THREE answers from the box and write the correct letter,
A-E, next to questions 11-13

> **A** electricity indicator
> **B** on/off switch
> **C** reset button
> **D** time control
> **E** warning indicator

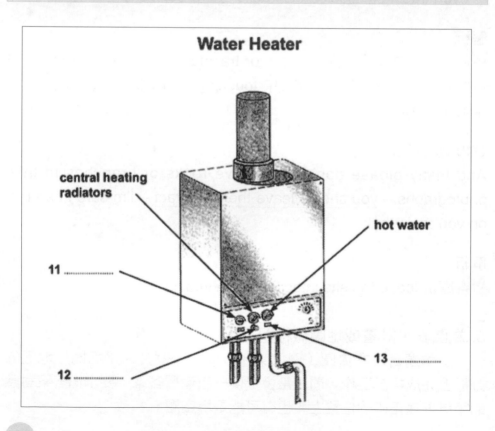

Water Heater

central heating radiators

hot water

11 ....

12 ....

13 ....

Q11-Q13 聽力原文：

In the upstairs cupboard, you'll find the water heater. You'll see three main controls on the left at the bottom of the heater. <u>The first one – the round one on the far left – is the most important one for the heating and hot water. It's the main control switch.</u> Make sure it's in the 'on' position. The switch itself doesn't light up, but the little square below will be black if the switch is 'off'. That's probably what's happened - it's got switched off by mistake. The middle one of these three controls – you'll see it's slightly larger than the first one- -controls the radiator. If you fell cold while you're there and need the radiators on, this needs to be turned to maximum. The last of the three controls - the one on the right – is usually on about a number four setting which for the water in the taps is usually quite hot enough.

<u>Below the heating controls in the middle is a small round plastic button</u>, if there isn't enough water in the pipes, sometimes the heater goes off, if this happens <u>you'll need to press this button to reset the heater.</u> Hold it on for about five seconds and the heater should come on again. then there is <u>a little square indicator under the third knob that's a kind of alarm light</u>. It'll flash if you need to rest the heater.

解析

題目圖形是一台機器，其中三個挖空處被提供了五個可選擇答案。聽力原文的先回答了加熱器不工作的問題，也對整個 heater 做了描述。在機器的左下方有幾個主要的控制按鈕和指示燈，左邊圓形第一個是 the main control switch，the one for the heating and hot water。五個選項裡沒有 the main control switch 這一項，原文補充說 Make sure it's in the 'on' position，可見主開關也是加熱器的 ON/

OFF switch，這是箭頭指向的 Q11 的位置，因而 Q11 答案為 B。中間和右邊的 switch 在圖中已經給出描述，分別為 radiator control 和 hot water control。Q12 箭頭指向 below the heating controls in the middle，用原文中這個定位句找到 Q12 的答案，press this button to reset the heater，與選項 C reset button 一致。Q13 是 a little square indicator under the third knob that's a kind of alarm light，選項 E warning indicator 是 alarm light 相同意義。

題目範例 **2**

Cambridge IELTS 8 Test 2 LISTENNING SECTION 2

Question 12-14
Label the plan below.
Write **NO MORE THAN TWO WORDS** for each answer.

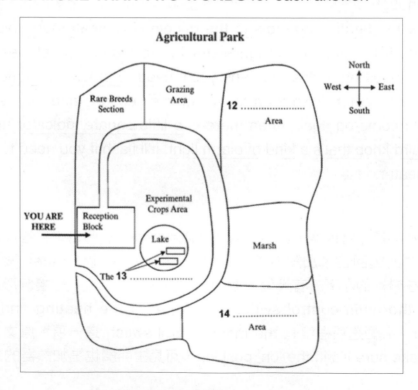

Q12-Q14 聽力原文：

　　Let's start by seeing what there is to do. As you can see here on our giant wall plan, we are now situated in the Reception block... here. As you walk out of the main door into the park there is a path you can follow. If you follow this route you will immediately come into the Rare Breeds section, where we keep a wild variety of animals which I shall be telling you a little more about later. Next to this... moving east... is the large grazing area for the rare breeds. Then further east... in the largest section of our Park is the <u>Forest Area</u>. South of the grazing area and in fact next to the Reception block is our Experimental Crop Area. In the middle of the Park... this circular area is out lake... These two small rectangular shapes here... are the <u>Fish Farms</u> where we rear fish for sale. To the east of those is the marsh area which attracts a great many migrant birds. In the south-eastern corner, beyond the marsh, is our <u>Market Garden</u> area, growing vegetables and flowers.

解析

聽力原文介紹農業園的平面圖，可以依據錄音中的關鍵字對應平面圖中的位置寫下正確答案。每一個 area 的位置，原文中都有具體指示方位的描述如：there is a path you can follow... follow this route you will immediately come into... next to this... then further east... south of the grazing area... in the middle of the Park... to the east of those... in the south-eastern corner。Q12 是進入園區後的第三個區域，位在 rare breeds section 和 grazing area 的東面，then further east... in the largest section of our Park is the Forest Area，答案為 Forest。Q13 是湖中兩個長方形的區域，原文為：these two small rectangular shapes here... are the Fish Farms，題目要求答案不超過兩個字，正確回答為 Fish Farms。Q14 的位置原文有精確表述：

in the south-eastern corner, beyond the marsh，答案為 Market Garden。圖表中的所有名詞都是首字母大寫，答案也必須符合同樣的格式。

題目範例 3

Cambridge IELTS 9 Test 2 LISTENNING SECTION 2

Question 17-20

Label the map below.

Write the correct letter, **A-I**, next to questions 17-20.

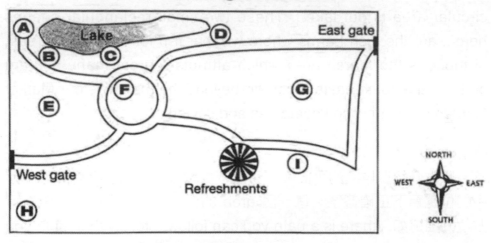

Hinchingbrooke Park

⑰ bird hide_____

⑱ dog-walking area

⑲ flower garden_____

⑳ wooded area_____

Q17-Q20 聽力原文：

And finally I'd like to tell you about our new wildlife area, Hinchingbrooke Park, which will be opened to the public next month. This slide doesn't really indicate hoe big it is, but anyway, you can see the two gates into the park, and the main paths. As you can see, there's a lake in the northwest of the park, with <u>a bird hide to the west of it, at the end of a path.</u> So it'll be a nice quiet place for watching the birds on the lake.

Finally close to where refreshments are available, <u>there's a dog-walking area in the southern part of the park,</u> leading off from the path. And if you just want to sit and relax, you can go to <u>the flower garden; that's the circular area on the map surrounded by paths.</u> And finally, there's <u>a wooded area in the western section of the park, between two paths.</u> Okay, that's enough from me, so let's go on to...

解析

這一題要求把區塊的名稱放入地圖正確的位置，關鍵字就是在聽力原文中聽到這些 area 的名字，並留意每一個位置的描述。Q17 有標示句 there's a lake in the northwest of the park，下面才説到 with a bird hide to the west of it, at the end of a path 標示 bird hide 位於湖西邊小路盡頭，答案為 A。Q18 也有直接説明 close to where refreshments are available, there's a dog-walking area in the southern part of the park，dog-walking 的區塊距離 refreshments 不遠，在公園的南邊，所以是 I。Q19 The flower garden; that's the circular area on the map surrounded by paths 是地圖中間被小路環繞的環形區塊 F。Q20 there's a wooded area in the western section of the park, between two paths，wooded area 則是公園西側兩條路之間的 E。

6. 分類／配對題

這兩種類型的題目分別是按照要求對聽力內容做分類、以及將聽力中出現的內容與題目中出現的內容進行配對，著重考察的是對細節的理解能力。題目的順序與聽力原文播放順序相同，只須準確定位正確答案並紀錄下來，不需要做大量記憶。

題目範例 1

Cambridge IELTS 10 Test 2 LISTENNING SECTION 2

Question 15-20

Which feature is related to each of the following areas of the world represented in then playground?

Choose **SIX** answers from the box and write the correct letter, **A-I**, next to questions 15-20.

Features
A ancient forts
B waterways
C ice and snow
D jewels
E local animals
F mountains
G music and film
H space travel
I volcanoes

Areas of the world

⑮ Asia_____

⑯ Antarctica_____

⑰ South America_____

⑱ North America_____

⑲ Europe_____

148

⑳ Africa_____

Q15 - Q20 聽力原文：

And now, moving on to the Central park Playground, which we're pleased to announce has just won the Douglas Award for safety: the news came through only last week. The unique design is based on the concept of the Global Village, with the playground being divided into six areas showing different parts of the world – each with a representative feature. For example, there is a section on Asia, and this is represented by rides and equipment in the shape of snakes, orang-utans, tigers and so on – fauna native to the forests of the region. Moving south to the Antarctic – we couldn't run to an ice rink I'm afraid but opted instead for climbing blocks in the shapes of mountains – I thought they could have had sliders for the glaciers but the designers did want to avoid being too literal! Then on to South America – and here the theme is El Dorado – games replicating the search for mines full of precious stones. And then moving up to North America, here there was considerable debate – I know the contribution of cinema and jazz was considered but the designers finally opted for rockets and the international Space Stations. Eastwards to Europe then, and perhaps then most traditional choice of all the areas: medieval castles and other fortifications. Then last, but not least, moving south to Africa and a whole set of wonderful mosaics and trails to represent the great rivers of this fascinating and varied continent.

解析

這一題是一個遊樂場按照各大洲名稱分區，題目要求找到遊樂場中每一大洲匹配的特徵。在聽力播放前應仔細閱讀 features 部分，以便聽力原文中出現同義替換時快速找到正確答案。Q15 亞洲的特性原文的描述是 section on Asia... represented by rides and equipment in the shape of snakes, orang-utans, tigers and so on – fauna native to the forests of the region，是各種動物型態的遊樂設施，其中 orang-utans（紅毛猩猩）、fauna（動物群）可能是生字，但不影響整句的理解。可以靠 snakes、tigers 判斷是動物相關的答案，而 native to the forests of the region 是 local 的意思，所以 Q15 為 E local animals。Q16 北極洲：we couldn't run to an ice rink I'm afraid but opted instead for climbing blocks in the shapes of mountains，沒辦法建滑冰場但做了可以爬的玩具山，答案為 F mountains。Q17 南美洲的主題是 El Dorado – games replicating the search for mines full of precious stones。El Dorado 是南美洲印加帝國傳説中的黃金城，在這個遊樂場它代表南美洲的特徵，是一個模擬的尋寶遊戲，D jewels 符合 precious stones 的描述。Q18 北美洲是在諸多選項中抉擇：I know the contribution of cinema and jazz was considered but the designers finally opted for rockets and the international Space Stations。答案不是 G music and film 而是 H space travel。Q19 歐洲選取了傳統的建築 medieval castles and other fortifications 中世紀的城堡和防禦工事，選項 A ancient fort 是正確選擇，fort、fortification 都是堡壘和要塞的意思，如果不知道這個單字，也可以通過 traditional choice、medieval 與 ancient 匹配，得到 A 選項。Q20 非洲 Africa and a whole set of wonderful mosaics and trails to represent the great rivers of this fascinating and varied continent，用馬賽克鋪路表現這個大洲的河流，B 選項的 waterways 對應關鍵字 rivers 是正確答案。

題目範例 2

Cambridge IELTS 10 Test 3 LISTENNING SECTION 3

Question 26-30

What action is needed for the following stages in doing the 'year abroad' option?

Choose **FIVE** answers from the box and write the correct letter, **A-G**, next to question 26-30.

Action
A be on time
B get a letter of recommendation
C plan for the final year
D make sure the institution's focus is relevant
E show ability in Theatre Studies
F make travel arrangements and bookings
G ask for help

Stages in doing the 'year abroad' option

㉖ in the second year of the course

㉗ when first choosing where to go

㉘ when sending in your choices＿＿＿＿＿＿＿＿

㉙ when writing your personal statement＿＿＿＿＿＿

㉚ when doing the year abroad＿＿＿＿＿＿＿＿

Q26 聽力原文：

ROB：But while you're here, Mia, I wanted to ask you about the year abroad option. Would you recommend doing that?

MIA：Yes, definitely. It's fantastic chance to study I another country for a year.

ROB：I think I'd like to do it, but it looks very competitive – there's only a limited number of places.

MIA：Yes, so next year when you are in the second year of the course, you need to work very hard in all your theatre studies modules. Only students with good marks get places – you have to prove that you know your subject really well.

解析

全篇主題是申請海外交換學生，這一組配對題目要求回答在每一階段要對應怎樣的行為。先閱讀 action 的 7 種選擇，分別是 on time, recommendation letter, final year plan, the focus is relevant, show ability, travel arrangement 和 ask for help。Q26 問課程的第二年需要做什麼，定位句是 next year when you are in the second year of the course, 應當做的是：you need to work very hard in all your theatre studies modules. Only students with good marks get places – you have to prove that you know your subject really well。必須努力學習，只有成績優異的學生才能成功申請，需要證明自己學業精通，符合選項 E show ability in Theater Studies。

Q27/Q28 聽力原文：

ROB：Right. So how did you choose where to go?

MIA：Well, I decided I wanted a program that would fit in with what I wanted to do after I graduate, so I looked for a university with emphasis on acting rather than directing for example. It depends on you. Then about six months before you go, you have to email the scheme coordinator with your top three choices. I had a friend who missed the deadline and didn't get her first choice, so you do need to get a move on at that stage. You'll find that certain places are very popular with everyone.

解析

Q27 選擇去哪裏時，定位句是 Rob 的問題 how did you choose where to go?回答是一個舉例：I decided I wanted a program that would fit in with what I wanted to do after I graduate, so I looked for a university with emphasis on acting rather than directing。Mia 選擇的學校優長在於表演而非導演，目的是為了符合之後的就業需要。最接近這個意思的答案是 D Make sure the institution's focus is relevant。 Q28 遞出申請時則應當 A be on time，舉例是 Mia 的朋友錯過了截止期限而無緣首選學校。

Q29/Q30 聽力原文：

ROB：And don't you have to write a personal statement at that stage?

MIA：Yes.

ROB：Right, I'll get some of the final year students to give me some tips... maybe see if I can read what they wrote.

MIA：I think that's a very good idea. I don't mind showing you what I did. And while you're abroad don't make the mistake I made. I got so involved I forgot all about making arrangements for when I came back here for the final year. Make sure you stay in touch so they know your choices for the optional modules. You don't want to miss out doing your preferred specialisms.

解析

Q29 撰寫個人陳述時，get some of the final year students to give me some tips，向高年級學長徵詢意見，答案為 G ask for help。 Q30 在海外交換的一年裡要注意什麼，Mia 說她在海外忙到忘記了為自己回國後做安排，因為還有大學的最後一年，所以答案為 C plan for the final year。

Cambridge IELTS 10 Test 4 LISTENNING SECTION 3

Question 25-30

What source of information should Tim use at each of the following stages of the work placement?

Choose **SIX** answers from the box and write the correct letter, **A-G**, next to questions 25-30.

Sources of Information

A company manager

B company's personnel department

C personal tutor

D psychology department

E mentor

F university careers officer

G internet

Stages of the work placement procedure

㉕ obtaining booklet_____

㉖ discussing options_____

㉗ getting updates_____

㉘ responding to invitation for interview_____

㉙ informing about outcome of interview_____

㉚ requesting a reference_____

Q25 聽力原文：

LAURA：... You should start by getting their booklet with all the details – I expect you can download one from their website.

TIM：Actually, they've got copies in the psychology department –

I've seen them there. I'll just go to the office and pick one up.

解析
題目問的是 Tim 尋找工作實習的每個步驟分別需要從哪裏得到訊息。Q25 在哪裡拿到 booklet，答案為 D psychology department。

Q26 聽力原文：
LAURA：Right. And then if I were you, after I'd looked at it I'd go over all the options with someone...
TIM：I suppose I should ask my tutor's advice. He knows more about me than anyone.
LAURA：One of the career officers would be better; they've got more knowledge about the jobs market than your personal tutor would have.
TIM：OK...

解析
應當找誰 discuss options，Tim 說要徵詢 tutor 的意見，Laura 說 the career officers would be better，答案為 F university career officer。

Q27 聽力原文：
LAURA：And then I suppose you just sit back and wait till your hear something?
TIM：They told ne at the careers office that it's best to be proactive, and get update yourself by checking the website for new placement alerts. Your mentor is supposed to keep you informed, but you can't rely in that.

最新的情況需要 checking the website for new placement alerts，從 G internet 取得。

Q28 – Q30 聽力原文：

TIM：I don't suppose it's a good idea to get in touch with companies directly, is it?

LAURA：Not really... But it is the company who notifies you if they want you to go for an interview. You get a letter of invitation or an email from personnel departments.

TIM：And do I reply directly to them?

LAURA：Yes you do. STEP only gets involved again once you've been made a job offer.

TIM：Right... So once you've had an interview you should let your mentor know what the outcome is? I mean whether you're offered a job, and whether you've decided to accept it?

LAURA：That's right. They'll inform the careers office once a placement has been agreed, so you don't have to do that.

TIM：Is that all?

LAURA：More or less. Only once you've accepted an offer you'll probably have to supply a reference, because the placement will be conditional on that. And that's something you should ask your own tutor to provide. He knows about you academic ability and also about your qualities, like reliability.

解析

Q28 獲得面試邀請時，You get a letter of invitation or an email form personnel departments，B company's personnel department 是正確答案。Q29 面試之後，once you've had an interview you should let your mentor know what the outcome is，需要讓 E mentor 得知面試結果。Q30 接受一份工作後，once you've accepted an offer you'll probably have to supply a reference，這個人則是 your own tutor，答案為 C personal tutor。

題目範例 4

Cambridge IELTS 10 Test 3 LISTENNING SECTION 2

Question 16-20

Which dolphin does Alice make each of the following comments about?

Write the correct letter, **A**, **B**, **C** or **D**, next to question 16-20.

Dolphins
A Moondancer
B Echo
C Kiwi
D Samson

Comments

⑯ It has not been seen this year._____

⑰ It is photographed more than the others._____

⑱ It is always very energetic._____

⑲ It is the newest one in the scheme.

⑳ It has an unusual shape._____

聽力原文：

　　People can choose one of our dolphins to sponsor. They receive a picture of it and news update. I'd like to tell you about four which are currently being adopted by our members: Moondancer,

Echo, Kiwi and Samson. Unfortunately, Echo is being rather elusive this year and hasn't been sighted by our observers but we remain optimistic that he'll be out there soon. All the others have been out in force - Samson and Monndancer are often photographed together but it is Kiwi who's our real 'character' as she seems to love coming up close for the cameras and we've captured her on film hundreds of times. They all have their own personalities – Moondancer is very elegant and curves out and into the water very smoothly, whereas Samson has a lot of energy – he's always leaping out of water with great vigour. You'd probably expect him to be the youngest – he's not quite – that's Kiwi – but Samson's the latest of our dolphins to be chosen for the scheme. Kiwi makes a lot of noise so we can often pick her out straightaway. Echo and Monndancer are noisy too, but Moondancer's easy to find because she has a particularly large fin on her back, which makes her easy to identify.

解析

這一題要為一些特徵配對它們分別屬於四隻海豚 Moondancer, Echo, Kiwi and Samson 中的哪一隻。Q16 哪一隻今年都沒有被看到,聽力原文中的描述是 Echo is being rather elusive this year and hasn't been sighted by our observers,答案為 B。Q17 被拍照最多的是 Kiwi seems to love coming up close for the cameras, we've captured her on film hundreds of times,答案是 C Kiwi。答案句之前的描述 Samson and Monndancer are often photographed together,有 photographed 一字出現可能造成迷惑,所以需要特別留意問題問的是什麼。Q18 最有活力的一隻是,Samson has a lot of energy,其中 energy 和 vigour 對應題目中的 energetic,答案為 D。Q19 最新加入 sponsor 計畫的也是 D,Samson's the latest of our dolphins to be chosen for the scheme。Q20 外型特別的是 A Moondancer，因為 Moondancer... has a particularly large fin on her back, which makes her easy to identify。

題目範例 5

Cambridge IELTS 8 Test 2 LISTENNING SECTION 4

Question 37-40

Which statement applies to each of the following people who were interviewed by Shona?

Choose **FOUR** answers from the box and write the correct letter, **A-F**, next to questions 37-40.

> **A** gave false data
> **B** decided to stop participating
> **C** refused to tell Shona about their job
> **D** kept changing their mind about participating
> **E** became very angry with Shona
> **F** was worried about confidentiality

People interviewed by Shona

㊲ a person interviewed in the street_____

㊳ an undergraduate at the university_____

㊴ a colleague in her department_____

㊵ a tutor in a foreign university_____

Q37 聽力原文：

I thought you might also be interested in some of the problems I encountered in collecting my data. There were odd cased that threw me - one of the subjects who I had approached while he was out shopping in town, <u>decided to pull out when it came to the second round.</u> It was a shame as it was someone who I would like to have interviewed more closely.

解析

這幾題要配對的是 Shona 在收集資料時遇到的特殊狀況，在街上遇見的調查對象原文說法是 was out shopping in town，問題中則是相近意思的 in the street。這個人的問題是 decided to pull out when it came to the second round，在第二輪調查時決定退出，B 選項 decide to stop participating 是正確答案。

Q38 聽力原文：

And one of the first-year students I interviewed <u>wanted reassurance that no names would be traceable from the answers.</u> I was so surprised, because they think nothing of telling you about themselves and their opinions in seminar groups!

解析

an undergraduate 即原文中的 the first year student，這個學生 wanted reassurance that no names would be traceable from the answers，要求確保名字不會洩漏，擔心的是 confidentiality，答案為 F。

Q39 聽力原文：

Then, one of the people that I work with got a bit funny. The questions were quite personal and <u>one minute he said he'd do it, then the next day he wouldn't, and in the end he did do it.</u> It's hard not to get angry in that situation but I tried to keep focused n the overall picture in order to stay calm.

解析

Shona's colleague in her department 對應原文中的 one of the people that I work with。這個同事的問題是 one minute he said he'd do it, then the next day he wouldn't, and in the end he did do it，出爾反爾，搖擺不定。是答案中的 kept changing their mind。答案是 D。

Q40 聽力原文：

The most bizarre case was a telephone interview I did with a teacher at a university in France. He answered all my questions in great detail – but then when I asked how much access he had to dangerous substances <u>he wouldn't tell me exactly what his work involved</u>. It's a real eye-opener...

解析

另一個例子是國外大學的一位老師 a tutor in a foreign university／a teacher at a university in France。這位老師拒絕透露他的具體工作，wouldn't tell me exactly what his work involved。答案為 C，refuse to tell Shona about their job。

Part 3
口譯練習

Part 3
口譯練習

MP3-01

Interviewer: Could you please briefly describe why you are the best candidate for this job?

Interviewee: Well, I've been granted a master of business with a major in accounting and finance with high distinction; this gave me a sound foundation to start a career in auditing. I also have the certified information systems auditor credential, which matches your selection criteria. Not only this, I believe auditing best suits my personality since I have a rational nature. I'm very logical with advanced analytical skills; also good at math and statistics. Furthermore, my interpersonal and communication skills make me a good team member; I also played a leading role in several group activities. You can refer to my resume to see details. Auditing would enable me to fuse all these positive aspects of my personality together, so I believe myself a very competitive candidate.

中譯

面試官：可以請你簡單的描述一下為什麼你是這份工作的最佳候選人嗎？

面試者：嗯，我獲得了商科碩士學位並且是優秀畢業生，專業是會計和金融，這為我從事審計工作打下扎實基礎。而且我考取了信息系統審計認證證書，符合您的選拔準則。不僅如此，我相信審計非常符合我的個性，因為我很理性。我的邏輯和分析能力很好，也長於數學和統計。而且我的人際溝通能力讓我適於團隊，我也有領導團體活動的經驗，在我的履歷中有詳細描述。審計工作可以讓我融合運用很多自己的優勢，所以我相信自己是這個職位有競爭力的候選者。

Recall

Interviewer: Could you please briefly describe why you are the best candidate for this job?

Interviewee: Well, I've been granted a master of business with a major in accounting and finance with high distinction; this gave me a sound foundation to start a career in auditing. I also have the certified information systems auditor credential, which matches your selection criteria. Not only this, I believe auditing best suits my personality since I have a rational nature. I'm very logical with advanced analytical skills; also good at math and statistics. Furthermore, my interpersonal and communication skills make me a good team member; I also played a leading role in several group activities. You can refer to my resume to see details. Auditing would enable me to fuse all these positive aspects of my personality together, so I believe myself a very competitive candidate.

C-E

面試官：可以請你簡單的描述一下為什麼你是這份工作的最佳候選人嗎？

面試者：嗯，我獲得了商科碩士學位並且是優秀畢業生，專業是會計和金融，這為我從事審計工作打下扎實基礎。而且我考取了信息系統審計認證證書，符合您的選拔準則。不僅如此，我相信審計非常符合我的個性，因為我很理性。我的邏輯和分析能力很好，也長於數學和統計。而且我的人際溝通能力讓我適於團隊，我也有領導團體活動的經驗，在我的履歷中有詳細描述。審計工作可以讓我融合運用很多自己的優勢，所以我相信自己是這個職位有競爭力的候選者。

E-C

Interviewer: Could you please briefly describe why you are the best candidate for this job?

Interviewee: Well, I've been granted a master of business with a major in accounting and finance with high distinction; this gave me a sound foundation to start a career in auditing. I also have the certified information systems auditor credential, which matches your selection criteria. Not only this, I believe auditing best suits my personality since I have arational nature. I'm very logical with advanced analytical skills; also good at math and statistics. Furthermore, my interpersonal and communication skills make me a good team member; I also played a leading role in several groupactivities. You can refer to my resume to see details. Auditing would enable me to fuse all these positive aspects of my personality together so I believe myself a very competitive candidate.

話題二 Shadowing　　　　　MP3-02

Tom: I've spent a lovely holiday in Germany and found a very interesting thing. Here we see foreign movies on TV with subtitles; but in Germany they dubbed the soundtrack. No matter whether the movie is in English or French or Chinese, all the characters speak German.

Lisa: That's interesting. It must seem funny to see Tom

Hanks or Jackie Chan talking in German. But good for the German audience.

中譯

湯姆：我在德國過了一個開心的假期，而且發現一件有趣的事。我們在電視上看外國電影一般都是帶字幕的，但是在德國都是配音的。不論電影語言是英文、法文還是中文，所有的角色都講德文。

麗莎：真有趣！可以看 Tom Hanks 或是成龍講德文。不過對德國觀眾倒是很方便。

Recall

Tom: I've spent a lovely holiday in Germany and found a very interesting thing. Here we see foreign movies on TV with subtitles; but in Germany they dubbed the soundtrack. No matter whether the movie is in English or French or Chinese, all the characters speak German.

Lisa: That's interesting. It must seem funny to see Tom Hanks or Jackie Chan talking in German. But good for the German audience.

C-E

湯姆：我在德國過了一個開心的假期，而且發現一件有趣的事。我們在電視上看外國電影一般都是帶字幕的，但是在德國都是配

音的。 不論電影語言是英文、法文還是中文，所有的角色都
講德文。

麗莎：真有趣！可以看 Tom Hanks 或是成龍講德文。不過對德國觀
眾倒是很方便。

E-C

Tom: I've spent a lovely holiday in Germany and found a very interesting thing. Here we see foreign movies on TV with subtitles; but in Germany they dubbed the soundtrack. No matter whether the movie is in English or French or Chinese, all the characters speak German.

Lisa: That's interesting. It must seem funny to see Tom Hanks or Jackie Chan talking in German. But good for the German audience.

話題三 Shadowing

 *MP3-03*

Tom: I've just seen a BBC documentary about our food future and I was very impressed. Our current energy intensive agricultural system consumes too much energy. That's neither reliable nor cost effective. We might face a future where energy runs out, so it's urgent to change our current way into the energy sustainable agricultural system.

Lisa: Don't worry too much and just relax. It sounds ideal to do environmental friendly agriculture, but I doubt that will become reality. Humans are used to living in unsustainable ways. I think for most farmers at this stage, it's not profitable to change the way they are.

湯姆：我看了 BBC 一個關於未來食物的紀錄片，印象很深刻。我們現在的高耗能農業模式消耗太多能量，既不可靠也不划算。我們將來可能要面臨能源耗竭，所以把目前的農耕方式轉換為可以永續利用能源的農業模式就刻不容緩。

麗莎：不要過於擔心，放輕鬆吧。環境友善型農業聽起來很理想化，不過我懷疑它真的會實現。人們習慣了破壞生態的生活方式，我覺得目前對大多數農民而言，改變他們習慣的方式並無利可圖。

Recall

Tom: I've just seen a BBC documentary about our food future and I was very impressed. Our current energy intensive agricultural system consumes too much energy. That's neither reliable nor cost effective. We might face a future where energy runs out, so it's urgent to change our current way into the energy sustainable agricultural system.

Lisa: Don't worry too much and just relax. It sounds ideal to do environmental friendly agriculture but I doubt that will become reality. Humans are used to living in unsustainable ways. I think for most farmers at this stage, it's not profitable to change the way they are.

C-E

湯姆：我看了 BBC 一個關於未來食物的紀錄片，印象很深刻。我們現在的高耗能農業模式消耗太多能量，既不可靠也不划算。我們將來可能要面臨能源耗竭，所以把目前的農耕方式轉換為可以永續利用能源的農業模式就刻不容緩。

麗莎：不要過於擔心，放輕鬆吧。環境友善型農業聽起來很理想化，不過我懷疑它真的會實現。人們習慣了破壞生態的生活方式，我覺得目前對大多數農民而言，改變他們習慣的方式並無利可圖。

E-C

Tom: I've just seen a BBC documentary about our food future and I was very impressed. Our current energy intensive agricultural system consumes too much energy. That's neither reliable nor cost effective. We might face a future where energy runs out, so it's urgent to change our current way into the energy sustainable agricultural system.

Lisa: Don't worry too much and just relax. It sounds ideal to do environmental friendly agriculture but I doubt that will become reality. Humans are used to living in unsustainable ways. I think for most farmers at this stage, it's not profitable to change the way they are.

話題四 Shadowing

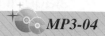

MP3-04

Tom: I'm hungry but it's only 4 o'clock. Shall we have afternoon tea before dinner? I will make a cheese board. I've newly bought Cheddar and Pecorino, and let's add some crackers, pastry, salami, apricot slices, grapes, and olive.

Lisa: Woo, delicious. I'm a bit peckish as well. Just that sounds bit more than a light dessert. I guess we might need to skip dinner after having that.

中譯

湯姆：我餓了，可是現在才 4 點。我們在晚餐前喝個下午茶怎麼樣？我來做一個奶酪拼盤。我剛買了 Cheddar 和 Pecorino 乳酪，再配一些餅乾、點心、香腸、杏乾、葡萄和橄欖。

麗莎：真美味！我也有點餓。不過聽起來比甜點的份量大，我猜吃過那些就不用再吃晚餐了。

Recall

Tom: I'm hungry but it's only 4 o'clock. Shall we have afternoon tea before dinner? I will make a cheese board. I've newly bought Cheddar and Pecorino, and let's add some crackers, pastry, salami, apricot slices, grapes, and olive.

Lisa: Woo, delicious. I'm a bit peckish as well. Just that sounds bit more than a light dessert. I guess we might need to skip dinner after having that.

C-E

湯姆：我餓了，可是現在才 4 點。我們在晚餐前喝個下午茶怎麼樣？我來做一個奶酪拼盤。我剛買了 Cheddar 和 Pecorino 乳酪，再配一些餅乾、點心、香腸、杏乾、葡萄和橄欖。

麗莎：真美味！我也有點餓。不過聽起來比甜點的份量大，我猜吃過那些就不用再吃晚餐了。

E-C

Tom: I'm hungry but it's only 4 o'clock. Shall we have an afternoon tea before dinner? I will make a cheese board. I've newly bought Cheddar and Pecorino, and let's add some crackers, pastry, salami, apricot slices, grapes, and olive.

Lisa: Woo, delicious. I'm a bit peckish as well. Just that sounds bit more than a light dessert. I guess we might need to skip dinner after having that.

話題五 Shadowing *MP3-05*

Mark: Hi everyone. We worked so hard in the past year and

we've made the most significant achievement in our company's history. May I show my deepest appreciation to all of you and wish everyone all the best! And I'm happy to announce that all of us will be rewarded an extra bonus. Let's toast for our outstanding team!

Stacy: Cheers! Thank you Mark, you are our best leader! We are all impressed by your willpower and insightfulness.

馬克：大家好，我們去年工作非常努力，達成了公司創辦以來最卓越的成績。我希望對諸位表達至深的感謝，祝各位一切順利！我很高興的宣布我們每個人都會得到額外獎金。讓我們為這個優秀的團隊乾杯！

史黛西：乾杯！謝謝你 Mark，你是我們最棒的領導者！我們都被你的意志力和洞察力折服。

Recall

Mark: Hi everyone. We worked so hard in the past year and we've made the most significant achievement in our company's history. May I show my deepest appreciation to all of you and wish everyone all the best! And I'm happy to announce that all of us will be rewarded an extra bonus. Let's toast for our outstanding team!

Stacy: Cheers! Thank you Mark, you are our best leader! We are all impressed by your willpower and insightfulness.

中譯

馬克：大家好，我們去年工作非常努力，達成了公司創辦以來最卓越的成績。我希望對諸位表達至深的感謝，祝各位一切順利！我很高興的宣布我們每個人都會得到額外獎金。讓我們為這個優秀的團隊乾杯！

史黛西：乾杯！謝謝你 Mark，你是我們最棒的領導者！我們都被你的意志力和洞察力折服。

E-C

Mark: Hi everyone. We worked so hard in the past year and we've made the most significant achievement in our company's history. May I show my deepest appreciation to all of you and wish everyone all the best! And I'm happy to announce that all of us will be rewarded an extra bonus. Let's toast for our outstanding team!

Stacy: Cheers! Thank you Mark, you are our best leader! We are all impressed by your willpower and insightfulness.

Derek: The school has created an online career portfolio for our new graduates. The portfolio is like a formatted C.V. with more specific details. Our university tenant pool is accessed by lots of cooperation, giving our students more chance to be hired.

Lisa: That's quite supportive for job hunting. The potential employees will easily see students' qualifications and experience.

中譯

德瑞克：學校為我們畢業生創建了一個線上的職業履歷，它像是你的履歷，有特定的格式和具體的細節。很多公司都瀏覽我們大學的人才儲備庫，所以我們學生有更多機會被雇用。

麗莎：這對找工作很有幫助，潛在的雇主可以很容易就看到同學們的各種資格和經驗。

Recall

Derek: The school has created an online career portfolio for our new graduates. The portfolio is like a formatted C.V. with more specific details. Our university tenant pool is accessed by lots of cooperation, giving our students more chance to be hired.

Lisa: That's quite supportive for job hunting. The potential employees will easily see students' qualifications and experience.

C-E

德瑞克：學校為我們畢業生創建了一個線上的職業履歷，它像是你的履歷，有特定的格式和具體的細節。很多公司都瀏覽我們大學的人才儲備庫，所以我們學生有更多機會被雇用。

麗莎：這對找工作很有幫助，潛在的雇主可以很容易就看到同學們的各種資格和經驗。

E-C

Derek: The school has created an online career portfolio for our new graduates. The portfolio is like a formatted C.V. with more specific details. Our university tenant pool is accessed by lots of cooperation, giving our students more chance to be hired.

Lisa: That's quite supportive for job hunting. The potential employees will easily see students' qualifications and experience

話題七 Shadowing

 *MP3-07*

Joey: The best thing I like in the new company is every week I could take two days work from home, which is quite convenient. Saved me the commute time.

Normally I have to drive one hour from home to work and when traffic is bad it takes much more.

Rita: You are lucky working in a cloud computing company. Salesperson like me could never imagine working from home. Hope it's not too late for me to plan for a career change.

中譯

喬伊：我最喜歡新公司的一點就是我每週可以有兩天在家工作，這很方便。節省了不少通勤時間。一般我從家裡開車到公司需要一小時，遇到塞車就要更久。

瑞塔：真好你在雲端計算公司上班，像我這樣的銷售人員可沒法想像在家上班。希望我現在轉換職業跑道還不算晚。

Recall

Joey: The best thing I like in the new company is every week I could take two days work from home, which is quite convenient. Saved me the commute time. Normally I have to drive one hour from home to work and when traffic is bad it takes much more.

Rita: You are lucky working in a cloud computing company. Salesperson like me could never imagine working from home. Hope it's not too late for me to plan for a career change.

C-E

喬伊：我最喜歡新公司的一點就是我每週可以有兩天在家工作，這很方便。節省了不少通勤時間。一般我從家裡開車到公司需要一小時，遇到塞車就要更久。

瑞塔：真好你在雲端計算公司上班，像我這樣的銷售人員可沒法想像在家上班。希望我現在轉換職業跑道還不算晚。

E-C

Joey: The best thing I like in the new company is every week I could take two days work from home; which is quite convenient. Saved me the commute time. Normally I have to drive one hour from home to work and when traffic is bad it takes much more.

Rita: You are lucky working in a cloud computing company. Salesperson like me could never imagine working from home. Hope it's not too late for me to plan for a career change.

話題八 Shadowing

 *MP3-08*

Tom: My sister is quite sleep-deprived recently, she just had a newborn and the baby never stays asleep for more than 2 hours. My sister has to wake up several times every night to feed and comfort the little one. She's asking when the baby will be able to sleep through the night.

Lisa: It will become better; babies will gradually sleep longer. Newborn's sleep cycle is different from ours maybe due to their rapid brain development; but most babies are capable of sleeping more than 8 hours when they turn somewhere between 4 to 6 months. Your sister can start to establish good sleep habits for her baby, like teaching baby to distinguish night from day, interact with him during the daytime and keep the noise and light low during night.

中譯

湯姆：我姐姐最近睡眠特別缺乏，她寶寶剛出生，小嬰兒一直睡不超過兩小時。我姐姐每晚都要起來好幾次餵奶安撫。她想問什麼時候小寶貝就可以睡過夜了？

麗莎：情況會變好，嬰兒會逐漸睡得久一些。新生兒的睡眠週期和我們的不同，這可能是由於他們在經歷大腦的快速發展。不過大多數寶寶到了 4 到 6 個月就都可以睡超過 8 小時了。你姐姐可以開始幫助寶寶建立睡眠習慣，像是教他區分白天和晚上，白天和他互動、晚上就把光線和聲音降到最低。

Recall

Tom: My sister is quite sleep-deprived recently, she just had a newborn and the baby never stays asleep for more than 2 hours. My sister has to wake up several times every night to feed and comfort the little one. She's asking when the baby will be able to sleep through the night.

Lisa: It will become better; babies will gradually sleep longer. Newborn's sleep cycle is different from ours maybe due to their rapid brain development; but most babies are capable of sleeping more than 8 hours when they turn somewhere between 4 to 6 months. Your sister can start to establish good sleep habits for her baby, like teaching baby to distinguish night from day, interact with him during the daytime and keep the noise and light low during night.

C-E

湯姆：我姐姐最近特別睡眠缺乏，她寶寶剛出生，小嬰兒一直睡不超過兩小時。我姐姐每晚都要起來好幾次餵奶安撫。她想問什麼時候小寶貝就可以睡過夜了？

麗莎：情況會變好，嬰兒會逐漸睡得久一些。新生兒的睡眠週期和我們的不同，這可能是由於他們在經歷大腦的快速發展。不過大多數寶寶到了 4 到 6 個月就都可以睡超過 8 小時了。你姐姐可以開始幫助寶寶建立睡眠習慣，像是教了他區分白天和晚上，白天和他互動、晚上就把光線和聲音降到最低。

E-C

Tom: My sister is quite sleep-deprived recently. She just had a newborn and the baby never stays asleep for more than 2 hours. My sister has to wake up several times every night to feed and comfort the little one. She's asking when the baby will be able to sleep through the night.

Lisa: It will become better; babies will gradually sleep longer. Newborn's sleep cycle is different from ours maybe due to their rapid brain development; but most babies are capable of sleeping more than 8 hours when they turn somewhere between 4 to 6 months. Your sister can start to establish good sleep habits for her baby, like teaching baby to distinguish night from day, interact with him during the daytime and keep the noise and light low during night.

話題九 Shadowing
 *MP3-09*

Lisa: Hello, may I make a reservation for five people this weekend? I would like to book the Fraser Island 2 day tour with the whale watching, and Saturday night we want to stay in the Kingfisher Beach Resort. Is there any vacancy please?

Receptionist: Let me check, 2nd to 3rd December…yes, we do have vacancies for the tour and the resort. It's 155 dollars per person and we now have seasonal promotion, so the price goes to 122. You have five people and you get a further 10% discount.

中譯

麗莎：您好，我可以預訂這週末五個人的行程嗎？我想訂 Fraser 島兩日遊含鯨魚觀賞，週六晚上我們想住在 Kingfisher 海灘度假中心。請問還有空位嗎？

接待員：我來查一下，12 月 2 日 3 日……有，兩日遊和住處都可以預訂。價錢是每個人 155 塊，我們現在有當季促銷所以現在價格是 122，你們五人預訂還有另外 10% 的優惠。

Recall

Lisa: Hello, may I make a reservation for five people this weekend? I would like to book the Fraser Island 2 day tour with the whale watching, and Saturday night we want to stay in the Kingfisher Beach Resort. Is there any vacancy please?

Receptionist: Let me check, 2nd to 3rd December…yes, we do have vacancies for the tour and the resort. It's 155 dollars per person and we now have seasonal promotion so the price goes to 122. You have five people and you get a further 10% discount.

C-E

麗莎：您好，我可以預訂這週末五個人的行程嗎？我想訂 Fraser 島兩日遊含鯨魚觀賞，週六晚上我們想住在 Kingfisher 海灘度假中心。請問還有空位嗎？

接待員：我來查一下，12 月 2 日 3 日……有，兩日遊和住處都可以預訂。價錢是每個人 155 塊，我們現仕有當季促銷，所以現在價格是 122，你們五人預訂還有另外 10% 的優惠。

Part 1

Part 2

Part 3

Part 4

Lisa: Hello, may I make a reservation for five people this weekend? I would like to book the Fraser Island 2 day tour with the whale watching, and Saturday night we want to stay in the Kingfisher Beach Resort. Is there any vacancy please?

Receptionist: Let me check, 2nd to 3rd December…yes, we do have vacancies for the tour and the resort. It's 155 dollars per person and we now have seasonal promotion so the price goes to 122. You have five people and you get a further 10% discount.

話題十 Shadowing *MP3-10*

John: The NetHealth database has crushed again. We need to call Matt to get the problem solved before patients come. It has become really unreliable after the last system update.

Rita: That's too bad. The third time this software has a problem in a single month! I'll call Matt now, and I do think we should purchase new software. Our patients' number has increased dramatically this year; it seems the current system couldn't process this much of data.

中譯

約翰：NetHealth 資料庫又壞掉了，我們得打電話給 Matt，在病人到
之前把它修好。上次系統更新後經常出問題。

瑞塔：真糟糕，這是一個月裡第三次出問題了！我現在就打給
Matt，而且我覺得應該購買新的軟體。我們的病人數量今年增
加很多，看上去目前的系統沒辦法處理這麼大量的資料。

Recall

John. The NetHealth database has crushed again, we need
to call Matt to get the problem solved before patients
come. It has become really unreliable after the last
system update.

Rita: That's too bad. The third time this software has a
problem in a single month! I'll call Matt now and I do
think we should purchase new software. Our patients'
number has increased dramatically this year; it seems
the current system couldn't process this much of data.

C-E

約翰：NetHealth 資料庫又壞掉了，我們得打電話給 Matt，在病人到
之前把它修好。上次系統更新後經常出問題。

瑞塔：真糟糕，這是一個月裡第三次出問題了！我現在就打給
Matt，而且我覺得應該購買新的軟體。我們的病人數量今年增
加很多，看上去目前的系統沒辦法處理這麼大量的資料。

John: The NetHealth database has crushed again. We need to call Matt to get the problem solved before patients come. It has become really unreliable after the last system update.

Rita: That's too bad. The third time this software has a problem in a single month! I'll call Matt now and I do think we should purchase new software. Our patients' number has increased dramatically this year; it seems the current system couldn't process this much of data.

話題十一 Shadowing MP3-11

Frank: Hi Sue, I haven't seen you and Peter for weeks. Have you been to your daughter's place again to visit her and the kids?

Sue: We didn't. We've just came back from an East Asia cruise. It was a wonderful experience. We stopped at Keelung, Hong Kong, Shanghai, Yokohama, and Jeju Island. Every time off board, we spent two to three days in those cities. That was the part I liked the most, we've experienced very kind local people and tried different Asian food. It's a pity we couldn't visit Shanghai because of the foggy weather, our boat did not manage to enter the harbor. But activities onboard were entertaining as well; so we've never felt bored.

Frank: Sounds good, just a bit tricky to catch up with bad weather. I went on a Caribbean cruise last year with several old friends and the Jamaica islands were ravaged by tropical storms several weeks ago. So when we off board we just visited several damaged sites. I hope the weather is nice to us when we go for a trip next time.

Sue: Yes, we should always hope for the best and prepare for the worst.

中譯

法蘭克：嗨 Sue，我好幾週沒看到你和 Peter 了。你們又去女兒那裡看她和孫子們了嗎？

蘇：沒有，我們剛從東亞的郵輪旅行回來。是很棒的經歷。我們停靠基隆、香港、上海、橫濱和濟州島。每次下船都在當地住兩三天。這是我最喜歡的，遇到不少善良的當地人，也吃了不一樣的亞洲食物。很遺憾我們沒有去上海玩，因為霧太大，船沒辦法入港。不過船上項目也很有趣，所以不會覺得無聊。

法蘭克：聽起來不錯，只是遇見壞天氣是有點棘手。去年我和幾個老朋友搭船去了加勒比海玩，幾週前牙買加的島嶼剛剛經歷了熱帶風暴的摧殘。所以我們下船後只看到幾處被毀的景點。希望我們下次出遊會遇上好天氣。

蘇：是咯，我們要有最好的希望，也要做最壞的打算。

Frank: Hi Sue, I haven't seen you and Peter for weeks. Have you been to your daughter's place again to visit her and the kids?

Sue: We didn't. We've just came back from an East Asia cruise. It was a wonderful experience. We stopped at Keelung, Hong Kong, Shanghai, Yokohama, and Jeju Island. Every time off board, we spent two to three days in those cities. That was the part I liked the most, we've experienced very kind local people and tried different Asian food. It's a pity we couldn't visit Shanghai because of the foggy weather, our boat did not manage to enter the harbor. But activities onboard were entertaining as well; so we've never felt bored.

Frank: Sounds good, just a bit tricky to catch up with bad weather. I went on a Caribbean cruise last year with several old friends and the Jamaica islands were ravaged by tropical storms several weeks ago. So when we off board we just visited several damaged sites. I hope the weather is nice to us when we go for a trip next time.

Stacy: Yes, we should always hope for the best and prepare for the worst.

C-E

法蘭克：嗨 Sue，我好幾週沒看到你和 Peter 了。你們又去女兒那裡看她和孫子們了嗎？

蘇：沒有，我們剛從東亞的郵輪旅行回來。是很棒的經歷。我們停靠基隆、香港、上海、橫濱和濟州島。每次下船都在當地住兩三天。這是我最喜歡的，遇到不少善良的當地人，也吃了不一樣的亞洲食物。很遺憾我們沒有去上海玩，因為霧太大，船沒辦法入港。不過船上項目也很有趣，所以不會覺得無聊。

法蘭克：聽起來不錯，只是遇見壞天氣是有點棘手。去年我和幾個老朋友搭船去了加勒比海玩，幾週前牙買加的島嶼剛剛經歷了熱帶風暴的摧殘。所以我們下船後只看到幾處被毀的景點。希望我們下次出遊會遇上好天氣。

蘇：是咯，我們要有最好的希望，也要做最壞的打算。

E-C

Frank: Hi Sue, I haven't seen you and Peter for weeks. Have you been to your daughter's place again to visit her and the kids?

Sue: We didn't. We've just came back from an East Asia cruise. It was a wonderful experience. We stopped at Keelung, Hong Kong, Shanghai, Yokohama, and Jeju Island. Every time off board, we spent two to three days in those cities. That was the part I liked the most, we've experienced very kind local people and tried different Asian food. It's a pity we couldn't visit Shanghai because of the foggy weather, our boat did not manage to enter the harbor. But activities onboard were entertaining as well; so we've never felt bored.

Frank: Sounds really good, just a bit tricky to catch up with bad weathers. I went on a Caribbean cruise last year with several old friends and the Jamaica islands were ravaged by tropical storms several weeks ago. So when we off board we just visited several damaged sites. I hope the weather is nice to us when we go for a trip next time.

Stacy: Yes, we should always hope for the best and prepare for the worst.

話題十二 Shadowing  *MP3-12*

Tom: How was your family Ekka day yesterday? Is this your first time visiting the agriculture show since you migrated to Australia?

Lisa: Yes, I haven't got a chance to go in previous years. It's really enjoyable on the whole. The kids were pretty happy. They spent long time with animals. The dogs' exhibition was my favourite. The thing I didn't find out so nice was the entrance fee. It was a bit expensive and nothing was included in the ticket price. We have to pay for extras on every activity inside. It's definitely much more expensive compared with other carnivals or theme parks.

Tom: I think so as well. I went to the Ekka last year and I don't plan to revisit in short future for the same reason. Their ice cream is the only thing I'm missing.

Lisa: Ha, girls like strawberry flavoured ice cream. My kids collected several showbags, I think there were only junk food and stationaries without any design; but they like them.

中譯

湯姆：你昨天的 Ekka 家庭日過得如何？這是你們移民到澳洲後第一次去農展會嗎？

麗莎：是啊，前些年我都沒有機會去。整體感覺是很有趣，孩子們很開心，他們花很長時間和動物相處。小狗展覽是我最喜歡的。我覺得不太好的是門票有些貴，而且什麼都不包括，裡面的所有項目都要另外付錢。確實比其他的嘉年華和主題公園貴很多。

湯姆：我也這麼覺得，我去年去了 Ekka，因為一樣的原因近些年也不打算再去。我唯一懷念的就是它的冰淇淋。

麗莎：哈，女生都喜歡草莓味道的冰淇淋。我小孩收集了很多展會包，我覺得裡面都是垃圾食品和不太有設計感的文具，不過他們喜歡。

Recall

Tom: How was your family Ekka day yesterday? Is this your first timevisiting the agriculture show since you migrated to Australia?

Lisa: Yes, I haven't got a chance to go in previous years. It's really enjoyable on the whole. The kids were pretty happy. They spent long time with animals. The dogs' exhibition was my favourite. The thing I didn't find out so nice was the entrance fee. It was a bit expensive and nothing was included in the ticket price. We have to pay for extras on every activity inside. It's definitely much more expensive compared with other carnivals or theme parks.

Tom: I think so as well. I went to the Ekka last year and I don't plan to revisit in short future for the same reason. Their ice cream is the only thing I'm missing.

Lisa: Ha, girls like strawberry flavored ice cream. My kids collected several showbags, I think there were only junk food and stationaries without any design; but they like them.

C-E

湯姆：你昨天的 Ekka 家庭日過得如何？這是你們移民到澳洲後第一次去農展會嗎？

麗莎：是啊，前些年我都沒有機會去。整體感覺是很有趣，孩子們很開心，他們花很長時間和動物相處 。小狗展覽是我最喜歡的。我覺得不太好的是門票有些貴，而且什麼都不包括，裡面的所有項目都要另外付錢。確實比其他的嘉年華和主題公園貴很多。

湯姆：我也這麼覺得，我去年去了 Ekka，因為一樣的原因近些年也不打算再去。我唯一懷念的就是它的冰淇淋。

麗莎：哈，女生都喜歡草莓味道的冰淇淋。我小孩收集了很多展會包，我覺得裡面都是垃圾食品和不太有設計感的文具，不過他們喜歡。

E-C

Tom: How was your family Ekka day yesterday? Is this your first timevisiting the agriculture show since you migrated to Australia?

Lisa: Yes, I haven't got a chance to go in previous years. It's really enjoyable on the whole. The kids were pretty happy. They spent long time with animals. The dogs' exhibition was my favourite. The thing I didn't find out so nice was the entrance fee. It was a bit expensive and nothing was included in the ticket price. We have to pay for extras on every activity inside. It's definitely much more expensive comparing with other carnivals or theme parks.

Tom: I think so as well. I went to the Ekka last year and not plan to revisit in short future for the same reason. Their ice cream is the only thing I'm missing.

Lisa: Ha, girls like strawberry flavoured ice cream. My kids collected several showbags, I think there were only junk food and stationaries without any design; but they like them.

話題十三 Shadowing　　　　　MP3-13

Stacy: Don't forget to vote today, the polling station will be closed at 6 pm.

Mark: I don't want to be bothered because I can't see any difference this vote will make. All the candidates say the same thing, and I believe they will perform the same as well. I can't tell the difference from those parties either.

Stacy: Well, you should exercise your democratic right, there used to be lots of sacrifices for gaining equally voting right to everyone. And it's not so bothering though; the polling station in our suburb is the state high school, which is just around the corner. Plus you will be fined 60 dollar if you don't go.

Mark: That's true, I will go as soon as I'm free this afternoon.

中譯

史黛西：別忘了今天去投票，投票站 6 點就關了。

馬克：我懶得去，因為我看不出來選舉能帶來什麼變化。所有候選人都說一樣的話，我相信他們做的也會一樣。我也分不出那些黨派有什麼區別。

史黛西：嗯，你還是應該用到你的民主權利，過去那麼多的犧牲就是為了爭取到每個人平等的投票權。而且也沒有多麻煩，我們這區的投票站就在不遠處的州立高中。並且不去投票你要被罰 60 塊。

馬克：沒錯，我下午有空時馬上就去。

Recall

Stacy: Don't forget to vote today, the polling station will be closed at 6pm.

Mark: I don't want to be bothered because I can't see any difference this vote will make. All the candidates say the same thing, and I believe they will perform the same as well. I can't tell the difference from those parties either.

Stacy: Well, you should exercise your democratic right, there used to be lots of sacrifices for gaining equally voting right to everyone. And it's not so bothering though; the polling station in our suburb is the state high school, which is just around the corner. Plus you will be fined 60 dollar if you don't go.

Mark: That's true, I will go as soon as I'm free this afternoon.

C-E

史黛西：別忘了今天去投票，投票站 6 點就關了。

馬克：我懶得去，因為我看不出來選舉能帶來什麼變化。所有候選人都説一樣的話，我相信他們做的也會一樣。我也分不出那些黨派有什麼區別。

史黛西：嗯，你還是應該用到你的民主權利，過去那麼多的犧牲就是為了爭取到每個人平等的投票權。而且也沒有多麻煩，我們這區的投票站就在不遠處的州立高中。況且不去投票你要被罰 60 塊。

馬克：沒錯，我下午有空時馬上就去。

E-C

Stacy: Don't forget to vote today, the polling station will be closed at 6 pm.

Mark: I don't want to be bothered because I can't see any difference this vote will make. All the candidates say the same thing, and I believe they will perform the same as well. I can't tell the difference from those parties either.

Stacy: Well, you should exercise your democratic right, there used to be lots of sacrifices for gaining equally voting right to everyone. And it's not so bothering though; the polling station in our suburb is the state high school, which is just around the corner. Plus you will be fined 60 dollar if you don't go.

Mark: That's true, I will go as soon as I'm free this afternoon.

話題十四 Shadowing *MP3-14*

Aaron: Hello, this is Aaron from the Runcorn Health Clinics. I just called to confirm if you have received my purchase order. I faxed it five minutes ago, but the pending light is still on in my fax machine. Not sure whether it got through or not.

Linda: Oh, sorry. Our fax machine is not working now. Sorry for the inconvenience. Would you mind to scan your order and send me via email? Our email address is sales001@brigmedical.com. I will process your order after I receive your email.

Aaron: Ok, I've written down your address, and I will send it to you in a few seconds. Just reconfirm before I send so you'll know that's from me. I will order 50 Clinell disinfectant wipes, two bottles of 4 Litre Clinidet instrument equipment detergents, and 20 surgical instruments.

Linda: Alright, got that. I will reply to you the invoice and process with your order in no time.

中譯

艾倫：你好，我是 Runcorn 診所的 Aaron。我打來確認一下你有沒有收到我的訂購單。五分鐘前有發傳真給你，可是我的傳真機現在還亮燈顯示未完成。我不太確定有沒有發出去。

琳達：對不起。我們的傳真機現在壞掉了。造成不便真是抱歉。你可以掃描訂單後寄郵件給我嗎？我們的電子信箱是 sales001@brigme dical.com。我收到信後就處理您的訂單。

艾倫：好，我抄下你的信箱了，等下就寄給你。發信之前再確認一下這樣你就知道那些是我訂的。我要訂購 50 組 Clinell 消毒紙巾、2 瓶 4 升裝 Clinidet 器材清潔劑和 20 個手術器械。

琳達：好的，收到。我會把發貨單據回信給你，馬上處理你的訂單。

Recall

Aaron: Hello, this is Aaron from the Runcorn Health Clinics. I just called to confirm if you have received my purchase order. I faxed it five minutes ago, but the pending light is still on in my fax machine. Not sure whether it got through or not.

Linda: Oh, sorry. Our fax machine is not working now. Sorry for the inconvenience. Would you mind to scan your order and send me via email? Our email address is sales001@brigmedical.com. I will process your order after I receive your email.

Aaron: Ok, I've written down your address, and I will send it to you in a few seconds. Just reconfirm before I send so you'll know that's from me. I will order 50 Clinell disinfectant wipes, two bottles of 4 Litre Clinidet instrument equipment detergents, and 20 surgical instruments.

Linda: Alright, got that. I will reply to you the invoice and process with your order in no time.

C-E

艾倫：你好，我是 Runcorn 診所的 Aaron。我打來確認一下你有沒有收到我的訂購單。五分鐘前有發傳真給你，可是我的傳真機現在還亮燈顯示未完成。我不太確定有沒有發出去。

琳達：對不起。我們的傳真機現在壞掉了。造成不便真是抱歉。你可以掃描訂單後寄郵件給我嗎？我們的電子信箱是 sales001@brigme dical.com。我收到信後就處理您的訂單。

艾倫：好，我抄下你的信箱了，等下就寄給你。發信之前再確認一下這樣你就知道那些是我訂的。我要訂購 50 組 Clinell 消毒紙巾、2 瓶 4 升裝 Clinidet 器材清潔劑和 20 個手術器械。

琳達：好的，收到。我會把發貨單據回信給你，馬上處理你的訂單。

E-C

Aaron: Hello, this is Aaron from the Runcorn Health Clinics. I just called to confirm if you have received my purchase order. I faxed it five minutes ago, but the pending light is still on in my fax machine. Not sure whether it got through or not.

Linda: Oh, sorry. Our fax machine is not working now. Sorry for the inconvenience. Would you mind to scan your order and send me via email? Our email address is sales001@brigmedical.com. I will process your order after I receive your email.

Aaron: Ok, I've written down your address, and I will send it to you in a few seconds. Just reconfirm before I send so you'll know that's from me. I will order 50 Clinell disinfectant wipes, two bottles of 4 Litre Clinidet instrument equipment detergents, and 20 surgical instruments.

Linda: Alright, got that. I will reply to you the invoice and process with your order in no time.

話題十五 Shadowing

Mark: You are out exercising your dog everyday. Hey, very energetic Shitzu, what's his name?

Lisa: He is Pingu with lots of energy. Yes he needs to be entertained and exercised daily; otherwise, he gets bored and chews whatever he finds. Yesterday he almost ate my mum's socks. I caught it before he swallowed it down; otherwise, I need to visit the vet again.

Mark: Someone says dogs have intelligence like three-year-old kids. If he doesn't get your attention, he might do something silly. I think now he looks like he wants one of us to throw that stick and play with him.

Lisa: Ok, now I'm going to throw the stick! Pingu, fetch!

中譯

馬克：你現在每天出來溜狗，真是隻有活力的西施犬，他叫什麼名字？

麗莎：他是精力充沛的 Pingu。是啊每天都要陪他玩和運動，不然他就會覺得無聊，見到什麼都要去咬。昨天他差點把我媽媽的襪子吃掉。他要吞下去之前被我發現了，不然又要去看獸醫了。

馬克：有人説狗狗有相當三歲孩童的智商。如果他沒有獲得你的關注，可能就會做些傻事。我覺得他現在看起來就想要我們投那根樹枝陪他玩。

麗莎：好，現在我要丟樹枝咯！Pingu 去撿回來！

Mark: You are out exercising your dog everyday hey, very energetic Shitzu, what's his name?

Lisa: He is Pingu with lots of energy. Yes he needs to be entertained and exercised daily; otherwise, he gets bored and chews whatever he finds. Yesterday he almost ate my mum's socks. I caught it before he swallowed it down; otherwise, I need to visit the vet again.

Mark: Someone says dogs have intelligence like three-year-old kids. If he doesn't get your attention, he might do something silly. I think now he looks like he wants one of us to throw that stick and play with him.

Lisa: Ok, now I'm going to throw the stick! Pingu, fetch!

C-E

馬克：你現在每天出來溜狗，真是隻有活力的西施犬，他叫什麼名字？

麗莎：他是精力充沛的 Pingu。是啊每天都要陪他玩和運動，不然他就會覺得無聊，見到什麼都要去咀嚼。昨天他差點把我媽媽的襪子吃掉。他要吞下去之前被我發現了，不然又要去看獸醫。

馬克：有人說狗狗有相當三歲孩童的智商。如果他沒有獲得你的關注，可能就會做些傻事。我覺得他現在看起來就想要我們投那根樹枝陪他玩。

麗莎：好，現在我要丟樹枝咯！Pingu 去撿回來！

E-C

Mark: You are out exercising your dog everyday. Hey, very energetic Shitzu, what's his name?

Lisa: He is Pingu with lots of energy. Yes he needs to be entertained and exercised daily; otherwise, he gets bored and chews whatever he finds. Yesterday he almost ate my mum's socks. I caught it before he swallowed it down; otherwise, I need to visit the vet again.

Mark: Someone says dogs have intelligence like three-year-old kids. If he doesn't get your attention, he might do something silly. I think now he looks like he wants one of us to throw that stick and play with him.

Lisa: Ok, now I'm going to throw the stick! Pingu, fetch!

Joey: Have you thought about how useful cell phones could be when you are traveling and facing a crisis situation? You can use it as your GPS, or torch. Not only that, I've read a news happened in Sri Lanka, a group of tourists hiked in remote area and stranded by tsunami, the authority located them by the signal from the cellphones.

Jenny: Woo, always taking a cellphone is a good habit then. A problem with smart phone is their batteries run out too quickly.

Joey: Yes, so we might have to take portable charging devices when we are travelling. Mobiles could be life saving.

Jenny: Not always. Last year a Taiwanese tourist dropped out of a dam near Melbourne, luckily a speedboat rescued her. Why was that? Because she was checking her Facebook while walking on the dam. People tend to shut off to the outside world whenever they are staring at their phones. So be aware of that as well.

中譯

喬伊：你有沒有想過當你在旅行時遇到危險，你的手機會多有用？你可以把它用作你的導航。不僅如此,我看了一條新聞,發生在斯里蘭卡,一組在偏僻地方遠足的遊客被海嘯困住了,救援人員靠他們手機發出的訊號找到了他們。

珍妮:看來時常帶著手機是個好習慣。智慧型手機的一個問題是電池耗用太快。

喬伊:是,所以我們出外旅行應該帶著便攜式充電器。手機可是會救命的。

珍妮:也不盡然,去年一個台灣遊客在墨爾本附近從水壩掉了下去,幸好她被一艘快艇所救。為什麼這樣?因為她一邊走在大壩上一邊看她的 Facebook。人們盯著電話時總會不自覺的切斷對外界的感知。所以這也是要注意。

Recall

Joey:Have you thought about how useful cell phones could be when you are traveling and facing a crisis situation? You can use it as your GPS, or torch. Not only that, I've read a news happened in Sri Lanka, a group of tourists hiked in remote area and stranded by tsunami, the authority located them by the signal from the cellphones.

Jenny: Woo, always taking a cellphone is a good habit then. A problem with smart phone is their batteries run out too quickly.

Joey:Yes, so we might have to take portable charging devices when we are travelling. Mobiles could be life saving.

Jenny: Not always. Last year a Taiwanese tourist dropped out of a dam near Melbourne, luckily a speedboat rescued her. Why was that? Because she was checking her Facebook while walking on the dam. People tend to shut off to the outside world whenever they are staring at their phones. So be aware of that as well.

C-E

喬伊：你有沒有想過當你在旅行時遇到危險，你的手機會多有用？你可以把它用作你的導航。不僅如此，我看了一條新聞，發生在斯里蘭卡，一組在偏僻地方遠足的遊客被海嘯困住了，救援人員靠他們手機發出的訊號找到了他們。

珍妮：看來時常帶著手機是個好習慣。智慧型手機的一個問題是電池耗用太快。

喬伊：是，所以我們出外旅行應該帶著便攜式充電器。手機可是會救命的。

珍妮：也不盡然，去年一個台灣遊客在墨爾本附近從水壩掉了下去，幸好她被一艘快艇所救。為什麼這樣？因為她一邊走在大壩上一邊看她的 Facebook。人們盯著電話時總會不自覺的切斷對外界的感知。所以這也是要注意。

E-C

Joey: Have you thought about how useful cell phones could be when you are traveling and facing a crisis situation? You can use it as your GPS, or torch. Not only that, I've read a news happened in Sri Lanka, a group of tourists hiked in remote area and stranded by tsunami, the authority located them by the signal from the cellphones.

Jenny: Woo, always taking a cellphone is a good habit then. A problem with smart phone is their batteries run out too quickly.

Joey: Yes, so we might have to take portable charging devices when we are travelling. Mobiles could be life saving.

Jenny: Not always. Last year a Taiwanese tourist dropped out of a dam near Melbourne, luckily a speedboat rescued her. Why was that? Because she was checking her Facebook while walking on the dam. People tend to shut off to the outside world whenever they are staring at their phones. So be aware of that as well.

話題十七 Shadowing

 MP3-17

Tom: The automated phone systems are so silly. I called the health insurance company to make a claim, and I have to listen to their greeting message for almost one minute. Pressed a key trying to skip this step, but the same paragraph just started to repeat.

Lisa: I can't stand them either. Last time I called the government for my family support payment and I listened to music for half an hour, finally they said all their customer assistants are busy, and I should ring back later. Luckily that was classical music.

Tom: Yes, they just made you listen to recorded voice messages one after another. I have to spend long time pressing keys to get the right option, sometimes get stuck on one step. When I am finally able to talk with a real person, I already felt a bit angry.

Lisa: That's so true, and the silliest thing is they ask you to answer questions verbally to an automated recorded voice, but their voice recognition technology is not so good. I have an accent and the machine can't distinguish it, I repeat a same word to the phone like an idiot.

中譯

湯姆：電話自動應答系統真的很蠢，我給健康保險公司打電話請款，得要花幾乎一分鐘聽他們的問候訊息。試著按鍵跳過這一步，卻讓同一段話重新開始朗讀。

麗莎：我也受不了電話自動應答。上次因為家庭輔助津貼打電話給政府，我聽了半小時音樂，最後他們説所有的接線員正在忙，請我稍後再撥。還好放的是古典音樂。

湯姆：是啊，他們讓你聽一條又一條預錄好的語音訊息。我不得不花很長時間選對選項，有時候還會在某一步卡住。當我終於可以和真人對話時已經覺得有點生氣了。

麗沙：確實如此，最傻的是讓你對著預錄的聲音回話，可是他們的人聲識別技術又不太好。我有口音，機器聽不懂，對著電話反覆説同一個字，像個傻瓜一樣。

Recall

Tom: The automated phone systems are so silly. I called the health insurance company to make a claim, and I have to listen to their greeting message for almost one minute. Pressed a key trying to skip this step, but the same paragraph just started to repeat.

Lisa: I can't stand them either. Last time I called the government for my family support payment and I listened to music for half an hour, finally they said all their customer assistants are busy, and I should ring back later. Luckily that was classical music.

Tom: Yes, they just made you listen to recorded voice messages one after another. I have to spend long time pressing keys to get the right option, sometimes get stuck on one step. When I am finally able to talk with a real person, I already felt a bit angry.

Lisa: That's so true, and the silliest thing is they ask you to answer questions verbally to an automated recorded voice, but their voice recognition technology is not so good. I have an accent and the machine can't distinguish it, I repeat a same word to the phone like an idiot.

C-E

湯姆：電話自動應答系統真的很蠢，我給健康保險公司打電話請款，得要花幾乎一分鐘聽他們的問候訊息。試著按鍵跳過這一步，卻讓同一段話重新開始朗讀。

麗莎：我也受不了電話自動應答。上次因為家庭輔助津貼打電話給政府，我聽了半小時音樂，最後他們說所有的接線員正在忙，請我稍後再撥。還好放的是古典音樂。

湯姆：是啊，他們讓你聽一條又一條預錄好的語音訊息。我不得不花很長時間選對選項，有時候還會在某一步卡住。當我終於可以和真人對話時已經覺得有點生氣了。

麗莎：確實如此，最傻的是讓你對著預錄的聲音回話，可是他們的人聲識別技術又不太好。我有口音，機器聽不懂，對著電話反覆說同一個字，像個傻瓜一樣。

E-C

Tom: The automated phone systems are so silly. I called the health insurance company to make a claim, and I have to listen to their greeting message for almost one minute. Pressed a key trying to skip this step, but the same paragraph just started to repeat.

Lisa: I can't stand them either. Last time I called the government for my family support payment and I listened to music for half an hour, finally they said all their customer assistants are busy and I should ring back later. Luckily that was classical music.

Tom: Yes, they just made you listen to recorded voice messages one after another. I have to spend long time pressing keys to get the right option, sometimes get stuck on one step. When I am finally able to talk with a real person, I already felt a bit angry.

Lisa: That's so true, and the silliest thing is they ask you to answer questions verbally to an automated recorded voice, but their voice recognition technology is not so good. I have an accent and the machine can't distinguish it, I repeat a same word to the phone like an idiot.

Mark: You look a bit tired, would you like a cup of coffee? My treat.

Jenny: Oh thank you! I went back home really late because I went to the Hyundai to watch the State of Origin. Such an excellent match and I'm really glad Queensland has won again. We went to a bar to celebrate after the match, so I struggled to get up to work today.

Mark: Envy you! The tickets have been sold out when I was going to book. I watched the game on TV last night. I'm Cheerful as well. I'm in the fan club of Queensland Maroons. Really happy for their victory.

Jenny: I'm not a fan of any team and generally I don't watch rugby; but I believe the State of Origin is Australian sport's greatest rivalry. The atmosphere in the stadium is so impressing.

中譯

馬克：你看起來有點累，要喝杯茶或是咖啡嗎？我來請。

珍妮：謝謝！我昨天回家很晚，因為我去了現代體育場看了 State of Origin 橄欖球賽。比賽超精彩，我很高興昆士蘭又贏了。我們賽後去了酒吧慶祝，所以今天早上費了很大力氣才起得來去工作。

馬克：好羨慕你啊！我預訂的時候票已經售罄。昨晚我在電視上看的
　　　比賽，我也很高興。我是昆士蘭 Maroons 隊球迷俱樂部成
　　　員，他們贏了我特別開心。

珍妮：我沒有加入任何球迷俱樂部而且我平常不看橄欖球，不過我覺
　　　得 State of Origin 是澳洲體育的最大對決，球場氛圍太令人印
　　　象深刻了。

Recall

Mark: You look a bit tired, would you like a cup of coffee? My treat.

Jenny: Oh thank you! I went back home really late because I went to the Hyundai to watch the State of Origin. Such an excellent match and I'm really glad Queensland has won again. We went to a bar to celebrate after the match, so I struggled to get up to work today.

Mark: Envy you! The tickets have been sold out when I was going to book. I watched the game on TV last night. I'm Cheerful as well. I'm in the fan club of Queensland Maroons. Really happy for their victory.

Jenny: I'm not a fan of any team and generally I don't watch rugby; but I believe the State of Origin is Australian sport's greatest rivalry. The atmosphere in the stadium is so impressing.

馬克：你看起來有點累，要喝杯茶或是咖啡嗎？我來請。

珍妮：謝謝！我昨天回家很晚，因為我去了現代體育場看了 State of Origin 橄欖球賽。比賽超精彩，我很高興昆士蘭又贏了。我們賽後去了酒吧慶祝，所以今天早上費了很大力氣才起得來去工作。

馬克：好羨慕你啊！我預訂的時候票已經售罄。昨晚我在電視上看的比賽，我也很高興。我是昆士蘭 Maroons 隊球迷俱樂部成員，他們贏了我特別開心。

珍妮：我沒有加入任何球迷俱樂部而且我平常不看橄欖球，不過我覺得 State of Origin 是澳洲體育的最大對決，球場氛圍太令人印象深刻了。

Mark: You look a bit tired, would you like a cup of coffee? My treat.

Jenny: Oh thank you! I went back home really late because I went to the Hyundai to watch the State of Origin. Such an excellent match and I'm really glad Queensland has won again. We went to a bar to celebrate after the match, so I struggled to get up to work today.

Mark: Envy you! The tickets have been sold out when I was going to book. I watched the game on TV last night. I'm Cheerful as well. I'm in the fan club of Queensland Maroons. Really happy for their victory.

Jenny: I'm not a fan of any team and generally I don't watch rugby; but I believe the State of Origin is Australian sport's greatest rivalry. The atmosphere in the stadium is so impressing.

話題十九 Shadowing *MP3-19*

Tammy: Morning, nice to meet you! I'm Tammy, and I haven't seen you before, are you new here?

Julia: Hi Tammy, I'm Julia, nice to meet you too. Yes, this is my second day in the company. I'm in the Research and Design Department. Everything is new to me, and I'm a new graduate. Hope you can give me some help if I have difficulty in my work.

Tammy: Sure, we should help each other in work and everything. Good to have you here. I'm doing the software testing. I'm sure we will collaborate well in the future.

Julia: Thank you so much and I believe so too. This is my

dreamed job, and I do hope I could contribute. Great to know you Tammy.

泰密：早安，很高興見到你！我是 Tammy，之前沒有見過你，請問你是新人嗎？

朱莉亞：你好 Tammy，我是 Julia，也很高興見到你。是的，今天是我在公司的第二天。我在研發部工作。我剛剛畢業，每件事對我來說都是新的。希望我遇到困難時可以得到你的幫助。

泰密：沒問題，我們應該在工作和其他事情上都相互協助。真好有你加入。我做軟體測試，相信之後我們一定會合作愉快。

朱莉亞：真的很感謝，我相信一定會。這份工作是我的理想工作，我很希望有所貢獻。認識你太好了 Tammy。

Recall

Tammy: Morning, nice to meet you! I'm Tammy, and I haven't seen you before, are you new here?

Julia: Hi Tammy, I'm Julia, nice to meet you too. Yes, this is my second day in the company. I'm in the Research and Design Department. Everything is new to me, and I'm a new graduate. Hope you can give me some help if I have difficulty in my work.

Tammy: Sure, we should help each other in work and

everything. Good to have you here. I'm doing the software testing. I'm sure we will collaborate well in the future.

Julia: Thank you so much and I believe so too. This is my dreamed job, and I do hope I could contribute. Great to know you Tammy.

C-E

泰密：早安，很高興見到你！我是 Tammy，之前沒有見過你，請問你是新人嗎？

朱莉亞：你好 Tammy，我是 Julia，也很高興見到你。是的，今天是我在公司的第二天。我在研發部工作。我剛剛畢業，每件事對我來說都是新的。希望我遇到困難時可以得到你的幫助。

泰密：沒問題，我們應該在工作和其他事情上都相互協助。真好有你加入。我做軟體測試，相信之後我們一定會合作愉快。

朱莉亞：真的很感謝，我相信一定會。這份工作是我的理想工作，我很希望有所貢獻。認識你太好了 Tammy。

E-C

Tammy: Morning, nice to meet you! I'm Tammy, and I haven't seen you before, are you new here?

Julia: Hi Tammy, I'm Julia, nice to meet you too. Yes, this is my second day in the company. I'm in the

Research and Design Department. Everything is new to me, and I'm a new graduate. Hope you can give me some help if I have difficulty in my work.

Tammy: Sure, we should help each other in work and everything. Good to have you here. I'm doing the software testing. I'm sure we will collaborate well in the future.

Julia: Thank you so much and I believe so too. This is my dreamed job, and I do hope I could contribute. Great to know you Tammy.

話題二十 Shadowing
MP3-20

Sue: Hi Kerry, we are going to hold a party at our backyard this Saturday evening. Sean has been promoted as his company's sales manager. Would you like to join us? You can bring your daughter along because our relatives will take their kids as well.

Kerry: Thank you, I'm glad to attend and big congratulations to Sean! He deserves that. I've seen him several times working after hours and sales is such a demanding job.

Sue: Yes, he is quite a workaholic. His company doubled its earning in last financial year and everyone in the sales department worked really hard. The party will start at 6:30 but if you can come early please arrive at 4pm. I will hold a one and half hour yoga course in the living room. It's free but you can drop a 5 or 10 dollar notes, that will be donated to the World Vision then. And kids can play together at afternoon teatime.

Kerry: Thank you a lot for your invitation Sue, that sounds great. We will come at 4 and after yoga I will see if I can give a hand for your party preparation.

中譯

蘇：嗨 Kerry，我們準備這週六晚上在家裡後院辦派對，慶祝 Sean 曾升成為他們公司的銷售部經理。你想要加入嗎？可以帶你女兒一起來，因為我們親戚的孩子們也會來。

凱瑞：謝謝，我很高興去參加，祝賀 Sean！這是他應得的，我好幾次都見到他加班，而且銷售是超級辛苦的工作。

蘇：是啊，他是個工作狂。他們公司上個財政年業績翻了一倍，他所在的銷售部每個人都非常努力工作。我們的派對 6:30 開始，不過如果你有空就請 4 點過來吧。我會在客廳教一個半小時瑜珈，參加是免費的，你也可以放 5 塊或 10 塊，我會一併捐個世界展望會。小朋友可以在下午茶時間一起玩。

凱瑞：非常感謝你的邀請 Sue，聽起來很棒。我們會 4 點到，瑜珈課後我再看能否幫你準備派對。

Sue: Hi Kerry, we are going to hold a party at our backyard this Saturday evening. Sean has been promoted as his company's sales manager. Would you like to join us? You can bring your daughter along because our relatives will take their kids as well.

Kerry: Thank you, I'm glad to attend and big congratulations to Sean! He deserves that. I've seen him several times working after hours and sales is such a demanding job.

Sue: Yes, he is quite a workaholic. His company doubled its earning in last financial year and everyone in the sales department worked really hard. The party will start at 6:30 but if you can come early please arrive at 4pm. I will hold a one and half hour yoga course in the living room. It's free but you can drop a 5 or 10 dollar notes, that will be donated to the World Vision then. And kids can play together at afternoon teatime.

Kerry: Thank you a lot for your invitation Sue, that sounds great. We will come at 4 and after yoga I will see if I can give a hand for your party preparation.

C-E

蘇：嗨 Kerry，我們準備這週六晚上在家裡後院辦派對，慶祝

Sean 晉升成為他們公司的銷售部經理。你想要加入嗎？可以帶你女兒一起來，因為我們親戚的孩子們也會來。

凱瑞：謝謝，我很高興去參加，祝賀 Sean！這是他應得的，我好幾次都見到他加班，而且銷售是超級辛苦的工作。

蘇　：是啊，他是個工作狂。他們公司上個財政年業績翻了一倍，他所在的銷售部每個人都非常努力工作。我們的派對 6:30 開始，不過如果你有空就請 4 點過來吧。我會在客廳教一個半小時瑜珈，參加是免費的，你也可以放 5 塊或 10 塊，我會一併捐個世界展望會。小朋友可以在下午茶時間一起玩。

凱瑞：非常感謝你的邀請 Sue，聽起來很棒。我們會 4 點到，瑜珈課後我再看能否為你準備派對幫的上忙。

E-C

Sue: Hi Kerry, we are going to hold a party at our backyard this Saturday evening. Sean has been promoted as his company's sales manager. Would you like to join us? You can bring your daughter along because our relatives will take their kids as well.

Kerry: Thank you, I'm glad to attend and big congratulations to Sean! He deserves that. I've seen him several times working after hours and sales is such a demanding job.

Sue: Yes, he is quite a workaholic. His company doubled

its earning in last financial year and everyone in the sales department worked really hard. The party will start at 6:30 but if you can come early please arrive at 4pm. I will hold a one and half hour yoga course in the living room. It's free but you can drop a 5 or 10 dollar notes, that will be donated to the World Vision then. And kids can play together at afternoon teatime.

Kerry: Thank you a lot for your invitation Sue, that sounds great. We will come at 4 and after yoga I will see if I can give a hand for your party preparation.

話題二十一 Shadowing

MP3-21

Annie: My parents are coming to visit Brisbane for a week; do you recommend anywhere interesting that I should take them to?

John: The city tour is a good one, and there is a free bus service for that. You can hop on and off at any stop of the red bus. Lots of nice sites along the route, the council hall, botanic garden, China town, etc. You could spend one day on that.

Annie: Thank you. Sounds like a very good option. Should I take them to the Australia Zoo? They might feel happy to see some typical Aussie animals.

John: I would recommend the Lone Pine Koala Sanctuary.

It's much closer to the city and you can take the cruise on the Brisbane River up there.

Annie: Cool, this one goes into my to do list as well. I also plan to go to the Mt Coot-tha and the national park in Tamborine Mountain. Then we may still have several days vacant.

John: If you go to the Tamborine Mountain, don't miss the Polish Cafe. They raised a big kookaburra, that's an Australian particular carnivorous bird. When it makes a sound, it very much resembles human laughter. Gold Coast and Sunshine Coast are worth visiting if you have extra days available, check what activities are over there during the days your parents are here, and they can take part in the true local culture.

中譯

安妮：我爸媽會來布里斯本旅行一週，你有推薦什麼有趣的地方嗎？我可以帶他們去。

約翰：市區遊覽還不錯，還有免費巴士可以搭，你可以搭紅色巴士在任意站上下車。這條線路上有許多不錯的景點，像是市政廳、植物園、中國城等。可以花一天在這項。

安妮：謝謝，聽起來還不錯。我要帶他們去澳洲動物園嗎？他們看到澳洲特別的動物應該會高興。

約翰：我比較推薦龍柏無尾熊保護區，離城區更近，而且你們可以乘船遊覽布里斯本河到達那裡。

安妮：好啊，這項也加入我的遊覽清單裡。我也計畫去庫薩山和坦莫寧山。這樣我們還有幾天有空。

約翰：如果你們去坦莫寧山的話，別忘了去那裡的波蘭咖啡廳。那家店養了一隻很大的笑翠鳥，是澳洲特有的一種肉食性的鳥，牠的叫聲聽起來很像人類的笑聲。如果你有時間，黃金海岸和陽光海岸也很值得一去。查一下你爸媽來玩期間有什麼活動，讓他們感受一下當地文化。

Recall

Annie: My parents are coming to visit Brisbane for a week; do you recommend anywhere interesting that I should take them to?

John: The city tour is a good one, and there is a free bus service for that. You can hop on and off at any stop of the red bus. Lots of nice sites along the route, the council hall, botanic garden, China town, etc. You could spend one day on that.

Annie: Thank you. Sounds like a very good option. Should I take them to the Australia Zoo? They might feel happy to see some typical Aussie animals.

John: I would recommend the Lone Pine Koala Sanctuary.

It's much closer to the city and you can take the cruise on the Brisbane River up there.

Annie: Cool, this one goes into my to do list as well. I also plan to go to the Mt Coot-tha and the national park in Tamborine Mountain. Then we may still have several days vacant.

John: If you go to the Tamborine Mountain, don't miss the Polish Cafe. They raised a big kookaburra, that's an Australian particular carnivorous bird. When it makes a sound, it very much resembles human laughter. Gold Coast and Sunshine Coast are worth visiting if you have extra days available, check what activities are over there during the days your parents are here, and they can take part in the true local culture.

C-E

安妮：我爸媽會來布里斯本旅行一週，你有推薦什麼有趣的地方嗎？我可以帶他們去。

約翰：市區遊覽還不錯，還有免費巴士可以搭，你可以搭紅色巴士在任意站上下車。這條線路上有許多不錯的景點，像是市政廳、植物園、中國城等。可以花一天在這項。

安妮：謝謝，聽起來還不錯。我要帶他們去澳洲動物園嗎？他們看到澳洲特別的動物應該會高興。

約翰：我比較推薦龍柏無尾熊保護區，離城區更近，而且你們可以乘船遊覽布里斯本河到達那裡。

安妮：好啊，這項也加入我的遊覽清單裡。我也計畫去庫沙山和坦莫寧山。這樣我們還有幾天有空。

約翰：如果你們去坦莫寧山的話，別忘了去那裡的波蘭咖啡廳。那家店養了一隻很大的笑翠鳥，是澳洲特有的一種肉食性的鳥，它的叫聲聽起來很像人類的笑聲。如果你有時間，黃金海岸和陽光海岸也很值得一去。查一下你爸媽來玩期間有什麼活動，讓他們感受一下當地文化。

E-C

Annie: My parents are coming to visit Brisbane for a week; do you recommend anywhere interesting that I should take them to?

John: The city tour is a good one, and there is a free bus service for that. You can hop on and off at any stop of the red bus. Lots of nice sites along the route, the council hall, botanic garden Chinatown, etc. You could spend one day on that.

Annie: Thank you. Sounds like a very good option. Should I take them to the Australia Zoo? They might feel happy to see some typical Aussie animals.

John: I would recommend the Lone Pine Koala Sanctuary.

It's much closer to the city and you can take the cruise on the Brisbane River up there.

Annie: Cool, this one goes into my to do list as well. I also plan to go to the Mt Coot-tha and the national park in Tamborine Mountain. Then we may still have several days vacant.

John: If you go to the Tamborine Mountain, don't miss the Polish Cafe. They raised a big kookaburra, that's an Australian particular carnivorous bird. When it makes a sound, it very much resembles human laughter. Gold Coast and Sunshine Coast are worth visiting if you have extra days available, check what activities are over there during the days your parents are here, and they can take part in the true local culture.

話題二十二 Shadowing
MP3-22

Rita: Parents and children living in my street have lived in fear for years and now we are finally at ease.

John: Why is that? What's the problem in your neighbourhood?

Rita: One of our neighbours raised a very fierce dog. It barks all the time whenever anyone walks pass by their door. The voice is quite loud and sounds scary. All kids are afraid of the dog. Last week the dog jumped out of the fence and almost bit a little boy on the road; luckily the owner held it up at the last second. But the kid was freaked out and had a fall. He had to be sent to hospital for a check.

John: That's awful! And why did you say your neighbourhood becomes relaxed?

Rita: That's because everyone complained about the dog after this incident. People from council came and assessed the situation; they declared it's inappropriate to keep such a fierce dog in the household. So the owner finally agreed to give the dog to his relative in the countryside.

John: I see. That's good for your suburb but good luck for people living close with his relative.

中譯

瑞塔：住在我們這條街的家長和小孩已經生活在緊張情緒裡好幾年了，現在終於鬆了一口氣。

約翰：為什麼會這樣？你家附近有什麼問題嗎？

瑞塔：我們的一個鄰居養了一隻很兇的狗。每次有人路過他們家門口牠都會叫。那個聲音很大，聽起來又有點恐怖。所有孩子都害怕那隻狗。上禮拜那隻狗跳過籬笆差點咬到一個路上的小男孩。幸好狗的主人在最後關頭把牠拉住了。但小孩被嚇壞了還摔倒，被送醫院檢查。

約翰：好糟糕！那你為什麼説你們那兒的人變輕鬆了？

瑞塔：是因為這件事發生後大家都抱怨那隻狗，政府工作人員來評估了狀況，他們説這麼兇的狗不適宜養在家裡。所以狗主人終於同意要把狗送給他住在鄉下的親戚。

約翰：原來如此。對你們那區是件好事，不過祝他親戚的鄰居好運。

Recall

Rita: Parents and children living in my street have lived in fear for years and now we are finally at ease.

John: Why is that? What's the problem in your neighbourhood?

Rita: One of our neighbours raised a very fierce dog. It barks all the time whenever anyone walks pass by their door. The voice is quite loud and sounds scary. All kids are afraid of the dog. Last week the dog jumped out of the fence and almost bit a little boy on the road; luckily the owner held it up at the last second. But the kid was freaked out and had a fall. He had to be sent to hospital for a check.

John: That's awful! And why did you say your neighbourhood becomes relaxed?

Rita: That's because everyone complained about the dog after this incident. People from council came and assessed the situation; they declared it's inappropriate to keep such a fierce dog in the household. So the owner finally agreed to give the dog to his relative in the countryside.

John: I see. That's good for your suburb but good luck for people living close with his relative.

C-E

瑞塔：住在我們這條街的家長和小孩已經生活在緊張情緒裡好幾年了，現在終於鬆了一口氣。

約翰：為什麼會這樣？你家附近有什麼問題嗎？

瑞塔：我們的一個鄰居養了一隻很兇的狗。每次有人路過他們家門口牠都會叫。那個聲音很大，聽起來又有點恐怖。所有孩子都害怕那隻狗。上禮拜那隻狗跳過籬笆差點咬到一個路上的小男孩。幸好狗的主人在最後關頭把牠拉住了。但小孩被嚇壞了還摔倒，被送醫院檢查。

約翰：好糟糕！那你為什麼説你們那兒的人變輕鬆了？

瑞塔：是因為這件事發生後大家都抱怨那隻狗，政府工作人員來評估了狀況，他們説這麼兇的狗不適宜養在家裡。所以狗主人終於同意要把狗送給他住在鄉下的親戚。

約翰：原來如此。對你們那區是件好事，不過祝他親戚的鄰居好運。

E-C

Rita: Parents and children living in my street have lived in fear for years and now we are finally at ease.

John: Why is that? What's the problem in your neighbourhood?

Rita: One of our neighbours raised a very fierce dog. It barks all the time whenever anyone walks pass by their door. The voice is quite loud and sounds scary. All kids are afraid of the dog. Last week the dog jumped out of the fence and almost bit a little boy on the road; luckily the owner held it up at the last second. But the kid was freaked out and had a fall. He had to be sent to hospital for a check.

John: That's awful! And why did you say your neighbourhood becomes relaxed?

Rita: That's because everyone complained about the dog after this incident. People from council came and assessed the situation; they declared it's inappropriate to keep such a fierce dog in the household. So the owner finally agreed to give the dog to his relative in the countryside.

John: I see. That's good for your suburb but good luck for people living close with his relative.

 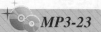

Annie: My friend's cat has given birth to three kitties and I plan to adopt one. I went to see them yesterday; they are so adorable and playful!

Mark: Another one? I think you've already had two cats at home, what breed are they then?

Annie: My cats are Tabby. Udon is silver and Mocha is brown, they both have black stripes and they are cousins. Udon and Mocha've been with me for 3 years. This time the little kitty is a British Shorthair; I haven't made him a name yet.

Mark: Good on you. Then there will be even more work to do, feeding them, chasing after them to tidy up, again and again.

Annie: That doesn't bother me. I really enjoy looking after them. The only inconvenience is when I go to somewhere else, I have to send them to pet's hotel. Just found one thing about cat is they seem to lose most of their playfulness when they get older. My two boys used to enjoy being teased with a piece of string and now they become so cool, especially

Udon, I can hardly find him.

Mark: Then I found out the reason why you want another kitty, get back the pleasant of their playfulness.

中譯

安妮：我朋友的貓生了三隻小貓咪，我打算領養一隻。昨天我去看了他們，特別活潑可愛。

馬克：又一隻？我知道你家已經養了兩隻貓了，是什麼品種來的？

安妮：我的貓是虎斑貓。烏冬銀色、摩卡棕色，兩個是表兄弟，都長黑色斑紋。烏冬和摩卡已經陪我三年了。這一次的小小貓是英國短毛貓，還沒有給取名字。

馬克：你太強了。之後就有更多照顧工作，要沒完沒了的餵牠們和追在牠們後面清理。

安妮：對我來說這沒關係。我真的很享受照顧牠們的過程。唯一不方便的是我如果要去別的地方，還要送牠們去寵物旅館。我發現貓咪長大後會失去小時候的活潑。我們家的兩隻曾經特別喜歡被我用繩子逗著玩，現在牠們都好酷，尤其是烏冬，我都找不到他。

馬克：我發現你要再養一隻小貓的原因了，想要重溫牠們的活潑可愛。

Annie: My friend's cat has given birth to three kitties and I plan to adopt one. I went to see them yesterday; they are so adorable and playful!

Mark: Another one? I think you've already had two cats at home, what breed are they then?

Annie: My cats are Tabby. Udon is silver and Mocha is brown, they both have black stripes and they are cousins. Udon and Mocha've been with me for 3 years. This time the little kitty is a British Shorthair; I haven't made him a name yet.

Mark: Good on you. Then there will be even more work to do, feeding them, chasing after them to tidy up, again and again.

Annie: That doesn't bother me. I really enjoy looking after them. The only inconvenience is when I go to somewhere else, I have to send them to pet's hotel. Just found one thing about cat is they seem to lose most of their playfulness when they get older. My two boys used to enjoy being teased with a piece of string and now they become so cool, especially Udon, I can hardly find him.

Mark: Then I found out the reason why you want another

kitty, get back the pleasant of their playfulness.

C-E

安妮：我朋友的貓生了三隻小貓咪，我打算領養一隻。昨天我去看了他們，特別活潑可愛。

馬克：又一隻？我知道你家已經養了兩隻貓了，是什麼品種來的？

安妮：我的貓是虎斑貓。烏冬銀色、摩卡棕色，兩個是表兄弟，都長黑色斑紋。烏冬和摩卡已經陪我三年了。這一次的小小貓是英國短毛貓，還沒有給取名字。

馬克：你太強了。之後就有更多照顧工作，要沒完沒了的餵牠們和追在牠們後面清理。

安妮：對我來說這沒關係。我真的很享受照顧牠們的過程。唯一不方便的是我如果要去別的地方，還要送牠們去寵物旅館。我發現貓咪長大後會失去小時候的活潑。我們家的兩隻曾經特別喜歡被我用繩子逗著玩，現在牠們都好酷，尤其是烏冬，我都找不到他。

馬克：我發現你要再養一隻小貓的原因了，想要重溫牠們的活潑可愛。

E-C

Annie: My friend's cat has given birth to three kitties, and I plan to adopt one. I went to see them yesterday; they are so adorable and playful!

Mark: Another one? I think you've already had two cats at home, what breed are they then?

Annie: My cats are Tabby. Udon is silver and Mocha is brown, they both have black stripes and they are cousins. Udon and Mocha've been with me for 3 years. This time the little kitty is a British Shorthair; I haven't made him a name yet.

Mark: Good on you. Then there will be even more work to do, feeding them, chasing after them to tidy up, again and again.

Annie: That doesn't bother me. I really enjoy looking after them. The only inconvenience is when I go to somewhere else, I have to send them to pet's hotel. Just found one thing about cat is they seem to lose most of their playfulness when they get older. My two boys used to enjoy being teased with a piece of string and now they become so cool, especially Udon, I can hardly find him.

Mark: Then I found out the reason why you want another kitty, get back the pleasant of their playfulness.

話題二十四 Shadowing *MP3-24*

Jeremy: Where are you off to? You look fantastic! I've never seen you wearing this outfit; it really suits you.

Linda: Thank you! I'm going to the city council to attend my colleague's wedding.

Jeremy: Congratulations to your college and why is at the city council? Isn't a wedding supposed to be in a church or somewhere?

Linda: Ahh, today they are going to the marriage registries to sign the legal document, and I am one of their witnesses. They will arrange the formal wedding ceremony another day. And that will be my big day as well, because I will make about 400 cupcakes for them.

Jeremy: Woo, that's a lot! I know you are good at baking, but 400 is a lot!

Linda: Yes, and my current place only has a small oven. But I will get everything prepared in advance.

中譯

傑瑞米：你要去哪裡呢？你看起來很漂亮！我沒有見過你穿這套衣服，跟你很搭。

琳達：謝謝！我要去市政廳參加同事的婚禮。

傑瑞米：恭喜你同事，不過為什麼是市政廳？婚禮不是都在教堂之類的地方舉行嗎？

琳達：喔，今天他們只是去簽法律文書註冊結婚，我是見證人之一。他們改天還會舉辦正式的婚禮。屆時也將是我的重要日子，因為我答應要幫他們做 400 個紙杯蛋糕。

傑瑞米：哇，很多呢！我知道你烘培很在行，不過 400 個真的很多。

琳達：是啊，而且我現在的住處只有一個小烤箱。不過我會提前準備好所有東西。

Recall

Jeremy: Where are you off to? You look fantastic! I've never seen you wearing this outfit; it really suits you.

Linda: Thank you! I'm going to the city council to attend my colleague's wedding.

Jeremy: Congratulations to your college and why is at the city council? Isn't a wedding supposed to be in a church or somewhere?

Linda: Ahh, today they are going to the marriage registries to sign the legal document, and I am one of their witnesses. They will arrange the formal wedding ceremony another day. And that will be my big day as well, because I will make about 400 cupcakes for them.

Jeremy: Woo, that's a lot! I know you are good at baking, but 400 is a lot!

Linda: Yes, and my current place only has a small oven. But I will get everything prepared in advance.

C-E

傑瑞米：你要去哪裡呢？你看起來很漂亮！我沒有見過你穿這套衣服，跟你很搭。

琳達：謝謝！我要去市政廳參加同事的婚禮。

傑瑞米：恭喜你同事，不過為什麼是市政廳？婚禮不是都在教堂之類的地方舉行嗎？

琳達：喔，今天他們只是去簽法律文書註冊結婚，我是見證人之一。他們改天還會舉辦正式的婚禮。屆時也將是我的重要日子，因為我答應要幫他們做 400 個紙杯蛋糕。

傑瑞米：哇，很多呢！我知道你烘培很在行，不過 400 個真的很多。

琳達：是啊，而且我現在的住處只有一個小烤箱。不過我會提前準備好所有東西。

E-C

Jeremy: Where are you off to? You look fantastic! I've never seen you wearing this outfit; it really suits you.

Linda: Thank you! I'm going to the city council to attend my colleague's wedding.

Jeremy: Congratulations to your college and why is at the city council? Isn't a wedding supposed to be in a church or somewhere?

Linda: Ahh, today they are going to the marriage registries to sign the legal document, and I am one of their witnesses. They will arrange the formal wedding ceremony another day. And that will be my big day as well, because I will make about 400 cupcakes for them.

Jeremy: Woo, that's a lot! I know you are good at baking, but 400 is a lot!

Linda: Yes, and my current place only has a small oven. But I will get everything prepared in advance.

話題二十五 Shadowing

 *MP3-25*

Mark: I've just been reading through the first draft of your dissertation.

Annie: I hope you didn't find too much wrong with it because I'm not sure whether my writing is on the right track.

Mark: Don't worry about it; I think your work is fantastic. The selection of your topic is excellent and the way you approach to the conclusion is quite creative.

Annie: Really? I'm glad that you give me such positive feedback. The first draft is just a rough structure, later I will focus on details and refine my findings. You made me reassured to continue with my writing.

Mark: You are so modest; just keep up with your high quality work. Your paper is really well organized and offers well thought out framework. I do recommend you to work into details on this paper and you should aim for a publication.

Annie: Thank you so much for your encouragement! I will do my best.

中譯

馬克：我剛讀過了你的論文初稿。

安妮：希望你不要發現太多錯誤，因為我不確定寫的是不是正確。

馬克：不要擔心，我覺得你的文章非常棒。你選了精彩的主題，而且得出結論的過程很有原創性。

安妮：真的嗎？真高興你給我這麼正面的評價。初稿只是大概的結構，之後我會專注寫好細節並且提煉我的調查結果。你讓我可以安心繼續寫下去了。

馬克：你太謙遜了，就繼續保持你的高品質工作吧。你的文章條理明晰，架構也經過了周詳的考慮。我認真建議你把細節寫好，以出版作為目標。

安妮：非常感謝你的鼓勵，我會盡全力。

Recall

Mark: I've just been reading through the first draft of your dissertation.

Annie: I hope you didn't find too much wrong with it because I'm not sure whether my writing is on the right track.

Mark: Don't worry about it; I think your work is fantastic. The selection of your topic is excellent and the way you approach to the conclusion is quite creative.

Annie: Really? I'm glad that you give me such positive feedback. The first draft is just a rough structure, later I will focus on details and refine my findings. You made me reassured to continue with my writing.

Mark: You are so modest; just keep up with your high quality work. Your paper is really well organized and offers well thought out framework. I do recommend you to work into details on this paper and you should aim for a publication.

Annie: Thank you so much for your encouragement! I will do my best.

C-E

馬克：我剛讀過了你的論文初稿。

安妮：希望你不要發現太多錯誤，因為我不確定寫的是不是正確。

馬克：不要擔心，我覺得你的文章非常棒。你選了精彩的主題，而且得出結論的過程很有原創性。

安妮：真的嗎？真高興你給我這麼正面的評價。初稿只是大概的結構，之後我會專注寫好細節並且提煉我的調查結果。你讓我可以安心繼續寫下去了。

馬克：你太謙遜了，就繼續保持你的高品質工作吧。你的文章條理明晰，架構也經過了周詳的考慮。我認真建議你把細節寫好，以出版作為目標。

安妮：非常感謝你的鼓勵，我會盡全力。

Mark: I've just been reading through the first draft of your dissertation.

Annie: I hope you didn't find too much wrong with it because I'm not sure whether my writing is on the right track.

Mark: Don't worry about it; I think your work is fantastic. The selection of your topic is excellent and the way you approach to the conclusion is quite creative.

Annie: Really? I'm glad that you give me such positive feedback. The first draft is just a rough structure, later I will focus on details and refine my findings. You made me reassured to continue with my writing.

Mark: You are so modest; just keep up with your high quality work. Your paper is really well organized and offers well thought out framework. I do recommend you to work into details on this paper and you should aim for a publication.

Annie: Thank you so much for your encouragement! I will do my best.

話題二十六 Shadowing

MP3-26

John: Have you ever counted how many hours you spend on your smartphone everyday? I just realised I've kept tapping my screen since I woke up today. It's crazy, just now I was browsing my phone but my mind was almost blank.

Annie: Same with you! I also check my phone compulsively. Too many things on the phone, checking emails, updating blog, watching Youtube, and lots of notifications and chatting to keep me busy.

John: Exactly, I'm always on social networks like Facebook, Twitter, Instagram, etc. I have spent too much time on replying to incoming messages.

Annie: I think what we have is the smartphone addiction. I never rely on my phone this much several years ago with my Nokia. But now the more I use it, the more often I feel the urge to look at the phone again. My battery never lasts for one day.

John: I'm even worse, sometimes I use my phone before knowing what I'm going to search. It's with me all the time. I've downloaded too many apps and my eyesight is getting worse quickly. We should reduce time spent on the smartphone.

Annie: I read an article and it said the smartphone posed constant interruptions and distractions to our daily life; the consequence is we couldn't maintain our attention, and our thoughts are always disturbed. If this situation lasts for a long time, our cognitive ability might be harmed.

John: Yes, we should suppress the curiosity of knowing everything and the time spent on smartphone should really be reduced.

Annie: Maybe the best thing we can do is being disciplined. It's no way to go back to the time where there isn't smartphone, but we could control our own mind. Let's try to wean ourselves away from it.

中譯

約翰：你有算過每天有幾個小時花在手機上嗎？我發現今天從醒來到現在我一直在滑手機。真恐怖，剛才我翻手機時候頭腦一片空白。

安妮：我和你一樣。我也無法控制地一直看手機。手機可以做太多事情了，我都忙於收發郵件、更新網誌、看 Youtube 影片，而且還有好多提醒和聊天。

約翰：就是，我時常待在社交網站上像是Facebook, Twitter, Instagram，也花了太多時間回復簡訊。

安妮：我覺得我們已經患上智慧型手機成癮症，幾年前我還在用諾基亞的時候從來沒有這麼依賴手機。現在我越是用它，就越覺得更需要頻繁看手機。電池電力沒有撐超過一天的。

約翰：我就更嚴重，有時候我還沒想清楚自己要搜尋什麼，就已經在用手機了。手機總是不離身。我下載了太多應用程式來用，我的視力變得更差。我們應該減低用手機的時間。

安妮： 我讀過一篇文章說，智慧型手機不斷地打斷日常生活、分散注意力，結果造成我們不能保持精力集中思緒總是受干擾，如果情況持續下去的話，我們的認知能力可能會受到影響。

約翰：是的，我們應當抑制住什麼事情都想知道的好奇心，減少用手機的時間。

安妮：或許我們應該讓自己更守紀律。雖然不可能再回到智慧型手機尚未問世的時代，但我們可以控制自己的頭腦。我們來試試不要用它好了。

Recall

John: Have you ever counted how many hours you spend on your smartphone everyday? I just realised I've kept tapping my screen since I woke up today. It's crazy, just now I was browsing my phone but my mind was almost blank.

Annie: Same with you! I also check my phone compulsively. Too many things on the phone, checking emails, updating blog, watching Youtube, and lots of notifications and chatting to keep me busy.

John: Exactly, I'm always on social networks like Facebook, Twitter, Instagram, etc. I have spent too much time on replying to incoming messages.

Annie: I think what we have is the smartphone addiction. I never rely on my phone this much several years ago with my Nokia. But now the more I use it, the more often I feel the urge to look at the phone again. My battery never lasts for one day.

John: I'm even worse, sometimes I use my phone before knowing what I'm going to search. It's with me all the time. I've downloaded too many apps and my eyesight is getting worse quickly. We should reduce time spent on the smartphone.

Annie: I read an article and it said the smartphone posed constant interruptions and distractions to our daily life; the consequence is we couldn't maintain our attention, and our thoughts are always disturbed. If this situation lasts for a long time, our cognitive ability might be harmed.

John: Yes, we should suppress the curiosity of knowing everything and the time spent on smartphone should really be reduced.

Annie: Maybe the best thing we can do is being disciplined. It's no way to go back to the time where there isn't smartphone, but we could control our own mind. Let's try to wean ourselves away from it.

C-E

約翰：你有算過每天有幾個小時花在手機上嗎？我發現今天從醒來到現在我一直在滑手機。真恐怖，剛才我翻手機時候頭腦一片空白。

安妮：我和你一樣。我也無法控制地一直看手機。手機可以做太多事情了，我都忙於收發郵件、更新網誌、看 Youtube 影片，而且還有好多提醒和聊天。

約翰：就是，我時常待在社交網站上像是Facebook, Twitter, Instagram，也花了太多時間回復簡訊。

安妮：我覺得我們已經患上智慧型手機成癮症，幾年前我還在用諾基亞的時候從來沒有這麼依賴手機。現在我越是用它，就越覺得更需要頻繁看手機。電池電力沒有撐超過一天的。

約翰：我就更嚴重，有時候我還沒想清楚自己要搜尋什麼，就已經在用手機了。手機總是不離身。我下載了太多應用程式來用，我的視力變得更差。我們應該減低用手機的時間。

安妮：我讀過一篇文章說，智慧型手機持續的打斷日常生活、分散注意力，結果造成我們不能保持精力集中，思緒總是受干擾，如果情況持續下去的話，我們的認知能力可能會受到影約翰：是的，我們應當抑制住什麼事情都想知道的好奇心，減少用手機的時間。

安妮：或許我們應該讓自己更守紀律。雖然不可能再回到智慧型手機尚未問世的時代，但我們可以控制自己的頭腦。我們來試試不要用它好了。

E-C

John: Have you ever counted how many hours you spend on your smartphone everyday? I just realised I've kept tapping my screen since I woke up today. It's crazy, just now I was browsing my phone but my mind was almost blank.

Annie: Same with you! I also check my phone compulsively. Too many things on the phone, checking emails, updating blog, watching Youtube, and lots of notifications and chatting to keep me busy.

John: Exactly, I'm always on social networks like Facebook, Twitter, Instagram, etc. I have spent too much time on replying to incoming messages.

Annie: I think what we have is the smartphone addiction. I never rely on my phone this much several years ago with my Nokia. But now the more I use it, the more often I feel the urge to look at the phone again. My battery never lasts for one day.

John: I'm even worse, sometimes I use my phone before knowing what I'm going to search. It's with me all the time. I've downloaded too many apps and my eyesight is getting worse quickly. We should reduce time spent on the smartphone.

Annie: I read an article and it said the smartphone posed constant interruptions and distractions to our daily life; the consequence is we couldn't maintain our attention, and our thoughts are always disturbed. If this situation lasts for a long time, our cognitive ability might be harmed.

John: Yes, we should suppress the curiosity of knowing everything and the time spent on smartphone should really be reduced.

Annie: Maybe the best thing we can do is being disciplined. It's no way to go back to the time where there isn't smartphone, but we could control our own mind. Let's try to wean ourselves away from it.

話題二十七 Shadowing　*MP3-27*

John: Have you seen the news photo, the three-year-old little Syrian asylum seeker lying lifeless on a

Turkish beach.

Victoria: Yes, it's heartbreaking. Seeing a little toddler lost his life on the way perusing a better life makes me cry.

John: This is not a single case, several tragedies had already happened this year. Months ago a boat carrying more than 700 refugees sank in the Mediterranean, most people drowned and only 28 survived from the disaster. Till September 2015, more than 2300 migrants died on their way to reach Europe this year.

Victoria: But for most refugees, it's still worth trying even though they know it could be a deadly voyage.

John: True, so far in this year, about 366,000 refugees had arrived in Europe from North Africa, more than half of them are from Syria. It's said in the news that the current conflict in Syria has created 4 million refugees.

Victoria: That's such a huge amount! The neighboring countries are under pressure of millions of refugees around the borders.

John: This time, the death of the little boy has raised international awareness. Many developed countries promised to accept more refugees. Germany made a commitment to process all asylum seekers' application; they plan to take 800,000 refugees this year.

Victoria: Thumbs up to Germany! A responsible country that takes international obligations. But still it's better to have a global resettlement program to solve the crisis in the long run.

(Reference: Only a global response can solve Europe's refugee crisis. by Phil Orchard)

中譯

約翰：你看了新聞圖片嗎？三歲的敘利亞小難民的遺體，在土耳其海灘上發現了。

維多利亞：是啊，真的很難過。一個小童為了尋求更好的生活卻失去了生命，看到這個讓我哭了。

約翰：這還不是個案，今年已經發生過幾次悲劇。幾個月前，一艘載著超過七百多難民的船在地中海沈沒，只有28人活了下來，大部分人都在這場災難中溺水死去了。截至2015年九月，有超過2300位移民死於去歐洲的路上。

維多利亞：但是對大多數難民來説，雖然知道可能是死亡之旅還是值得一試。

約翰：對，到目前為止，今年已經有大約36.6萬難民從北非到達歐洲，一半以上來自敘利亞。新聞說目前的敘利亞衝突已經造成了四百萬難民。

維多利亞：真是一個超大的數字！鄰國也受到邊境的百萬難民的壓力。

約翰：這一次小男孩的死被全世界關注，許多發達國家答應會接收更多難民。德國承諾了要處理所有避難者的申請，他們今年會接受八十萬難民。

維多利亞：德國好棒！是具承擔國際義務的負責國家。不過長久看來最好還是有全球性的安置計畫才能應對這次危機。

Recall

John: Have you seen the news photo, the three-year-old little Syrian asylum seeker lying lifeless on a Turkish beach.

Victoria: Yes, it's heartbreaking. Seeing a little toddler lost his life on the way pursuing a better life makes me cry.

John: This is not a single case, several tragedies had already happened this year. Months ago a boat carrying more than 700 refugees sank in the Mediterranean. Most people drowned and only 28 survived from the disaster. Till September 2015, more than 2300 migrants died on their way to reach Europe this year.

Victoria: But for most refugees, it's still worth trying even though they know it could be a deadly voyage.

John: True, so far in this year, about 366,000 refugees had arrived in Europe from North Africa, more than half of them are from Syria. It's said in the news that the current conflict in Syria has created 4 million refugees.

Victoria: That's such a huge amount! The neighboring countries are under pressure of millions of refugees around the borders.

John: This time, the death of the little boy has raised international awareness. Many developed countries promised to accept more refugees. Germany made a commitment to process all asylum seekers' application; they plan to take 800,000 refugees this year.

Victoria: Thumbs up to Germany! A responsible country that takes international obligations. But still it's better to have a global resettlement program to solve the crisis in the long run.

(Reference: Only a global response can solve Europe's refugee crisis. by Phil Orchard)

約翰：你看了新聞圖片嗎？三歲的敘利亞小難民的遺體，在土耳其海灘上發現了。

維多利亞：是啊，真的很難過。一個小童為了尋求更好的生活卻失去了生命，看到這個讓我哭了。

約翰：這還不是個案，今年已經發生過幾次悲劇。幾個月前，一艘載著超過七百多難民的船在地中海沈沒，只有28人活了下來，大部分人都在這場災難中溺水死去了。截至2015年九月，有超過2300位移民死於去歐洲的路上。

維多利亞：但是對大多數難民來説，雖然知道可能是死亡之旅還是值得一試。

約翰：對，到目前為止，今年已經有大約36.6萬難民從北非到達歐洲，一半以上來自敘利亞。新聞説目前的敘利亞衝突已經造成了四百萬難民。

維多利亞：真是一個超大的數字！鄰國也受到邊境的百萬難民的壓力。

約翰：這一次小男孩的死被全世界關注，許多發達國家答應會接收更多難民。德國承諾了要處理所有避難者的申請，他們今年會接受八十萬難民。

維多利亞：德國好棒！是具承擔國際義務的負責國家。不過長久看來最好還是有全球性的安置計畫才能應對這次危機。

E-C

John: Have you seen the news photo, the three-year-old little Syrian asylum seeker lying lifeless on a Turkish beach.

Victoria: Yes, it's heartbreaking. Seeing a little toddler lost his life on the way pursuing a better life makes me cry.

John: This is not a single case, several tragedies had already happened this year. Months ago a boat carrying more than 700 refugees sank in the Mediterranean. Most people drowned and only 28 survived from the disaster. Till September 2015, more than 2300 migrants died on their way to reach Europe this year.

Victoria: But for most refugees, it's still worth trying even they know it could be a deadly voyage.

John: True, so far in this year, about 366,000 refugees had arrived Europe from North Africa, more than half of them are from Syria. It's said in the news that the current conflict in Syria has created 4 million refugees.

Victoria: That's such a huge amount! The neighboring countries are under pressure of millions of refugees around the borders.

John: This time, the death of the little boy has raised international awareness. Many developed countries promised to accept more refugees. Germany made a commitment to process all asylum seekers' application; they plan to take 800,000 refugees this year.

Victoria: Thumbs up to Germany! A responsible country that takes international obligations. But still it's better to have a global resettlement program to solve the crisis in along run.

(Reference: Only a global response can solve Europe's refugee crisis. by Phil Orchard)

話題二十八 Shadowing

MP3-28

Rita: My brother went to the doctor for prescription again. He woke up with sore throat this morning and said he needs antibiotics.

Frank: Sorry to hear that. He'd better drink plenty of water and rest up. I think he may not need antibiotics since the sore throat could be caused by reasons other than bacteria infection. But the doctor will let him know.

Rita: I told him the same thing, but he wouldn't listen. I will get him to see you. You study medicine and your persuasion should be much more convincing. Last time he asked his GP to prescribe him with antibiotics and the GP did so.

Frank: Ha, what his GP did was not rare. I've just read an interesting survey about the antibiotics usage rate in Australia. It said nearly 60% of GPs have surveyed would prescribe antibiotics to meet patients' demands. Also two-thirds of the general public believed antibiotics help them recover quicker from colds, and even 20% of people expect antibiotics would treat viral infections.

Rita: This is really a misunderstanding. Antibiotics are overly used than they should be.

Frank: It's true. There are many inappropriate prescriptions of antibiotics. Antibiotics are useful to prevent serious infections and stop bad infections from getting fatal. But even when they are used for targeting bacterial infections, there are negative effects. The main reason is the medical knowledge these days could not distinguish which bacteria has caused the infection; without an accurate diagnosis, doctors have to use a broad-spectrum antibiotic which damages lots of good bacteria and harms patient's immune system and overall health.

Rita: And bacteria will upgrade with antibiotics.

Frank: Yes, antibiotic-resistant superbugs are spreading. Like MRSA, temporarily no medicine could defeat it. But in your brother's case, using antibiotics probably do him more harm than good.

(reference: When should you take antibiotics. by Matthew Cooper)

中譯

瑞塔：我哥哥又去找醫生開處方了。他今早起來喉嚨痛說他需要抗生素。

法蘭克：抱歉聽到他生病了，他最好多喝水、好好休息。我覺得他可能不需要抗生素，因為喉嚨痛或許不是細菌感染造成的，而是由於其他原因。不過這個醫生會告訴他。

瑞塔：我也是這樣和他說的，但是他聽不進去。我得讓他見見你，你學醫，講話更有說服力。上次他讓醫生開抗生素給他，醫生居然照辦了。

法蘭克：哈，那醫生的做法不稀奇。我剛剛讀過一份關於澳洲抗生素使用率的有趣調查，上面說接近六成接受調查的家醫師承認他們會根據病人的要求給他們開抗生素處方。而且大眾中有三分之二相信抗生素可以使他們從感冒中快速康復，甚至有兩成人相信抗生素可以治療病毒感染。

瑞塔：這確實是個誤解，抗生素被用過量了。

法蘭克：是啊，有很多抗生素處方都開的不太合適。抗生素對預防嚴重感染和防止致命感染很有效。但是即使是用於治療嚴重細菌感染，也有副作用。主要原因是當下的醫學知識還沒有辦法區分出是哪種細菌導致了感染，由於沒有精確的診斷，醫生只好用廣譜抗生素，這就會一併滅除體內的很多有益菌，損害病人的免疫系統和整體健康。

瑞塔：而且細菌也會跟著抗生素升級。

法蘭克：是啊，耐藥性的超級菌種在蔓延。像是金黃色葡萄球菌，目前就沒有藥物可以控制。不過像是你哥哥的狀況，用抗生素可能會弊大於利。

Recall

Rita: My brother went to the doctor for prescription again. He woke up with sore throat this morning and said he needs antibiotics.

Frank: Sorry to hear that. He'd better drink plenty of water and rest up. I think he may not need antibiotics since the sore throat could be caused by reasons other than bacteria infection. But the doctor will let him know.

Rita: I told him the same thing, but he wouldn't listen. I will get him to see you. You study medicine and your persuasion should be much more convincing. Last time he asked his GP to prescribe him with antibiotics and the GP did so.

Frank: Ha, what his GP did was not rare. I've just read an interesting survey about the antibiotics usage rate in Australia. It said nearly 60% of GPs have surveyed would prescribe antibiotics to meet patients' demands. Also two-thirds of the general public believed antibiotics help them recover quicker from cold, and even 20% of people expect antibiotics would treat viral infections.

Rita: This is really a misunderstanding. Antibiotics are overly used than they should be.

Frank: It's true. There are many inappropriate prescriptions of antibiotics. Antibiotics are useful to prevent serious infections and stop bad infections from getting fatal. But even when they are used for targeting bacterial infections, there are negative effects. Main reason is the medical knowledge these days could not distinguish which bacteria has caused the infection; without an accurate diagnosis, doctors have to use a broad-spectrum antibiotic which damages lots of good bacteria and harms patient's immune system and overall health.

Rita: And bacteria will upgrade with antibiotics.

Frank: Yes, antibiotic-resistant superbugs are spreading.

Like MRSA, temporarily no medicine could defeat it. But in your brother's case, using antibiotics probably do him more harm than good.

(reference: When should you take antibiotics. by Matthew Cooper)

C-E

瑞塔：我哥哥又去找醫生開處方了。他今早起來喉嚨痛說他需要抗生素。

法蘭克：抱歉聽到他生病了，他最好多喝水、好好休息。我覺得他可能不需要抗生素，因為喉嚨痛或許不是細菌感染造成的，而是由於其他原因。不過這個醫生會告訴他。

瑞塔：我也是這樣和他說的，但是他聽不進去。我得讓他見見你，你學醫，講話更有說服力。上次他讓醫生開抗生素給他醫生居然照辦了。

法蘭克：哈，那醫生的做法不稀奇。我剛剛讀過一份關於澳洲抗生素使用率的有趣調查，上面說接近六成接受調查的家醫師承認他們會根據病人的要求給他們開抗生素處方。而且大眾中有三分之二相信抗生素可以使他們從感冒中快速康復，甚至有兩成人相信抗生素可以治療病毒感染。

瑞塔：這確實是個誤解，抗生素被用過量了。

法蘭克：是啊，有很多抗生素處方都開的不太合適。抗生素對預防嚴重感染和防止致命感染很有效。但是即使是用於治療細菌感染，也有副作用。主要原因是當下的醫學知識還沒有辦法區分出是哪種細菌導致了感染，由於沒有精確的診斷，醫生只好用廣譜抗生素，這就會一併滅除體內的很多有益菌，損害病人的免疫系統和整體健康。

瑞塔：而且細菌也會跟著抗生素升級。

法蘭克：是啊，耐藥性的超級菌種在蔓延。像是金黃色葡萄球菌，目前就沒有藥物可以控制。不過像是你哥哥的狀況，用抗生素可能會弊大於利。

E-C

Rita: My brother went to the doctor for prescription again. He woke up with sore throat this morning and said he needs antibiotics.

Frank: Sorry to hear that. He'd better drink plenty of water and rest up. I think he may not need antibiotics since the sore throat could be caused by reasons other than bacteria infection. But the doctor will let him know.

Rita: I told him the same thing, but he wouldn't listen. I will get him to see you. You study medicine and your persuasion should be much more convincing. Last time he asked his GP to prescribe him with antibiotics and the GP did so.

Frank: Ha, what his GP did was not rare. I've just read an interesting survey about the antibiotics usage rate in Australia. It said nearly 60% of GPs have been surveyed would prescribe antibiotics to meet patients' demands. Also two-thirds of the general public believed antibiotics help them recover quicker from cold, and even 20% of people expect antibiotics would treat viral infections.

Rita: This is really a misunderstanding. Antibiotics are overly used than they should be.

Frank: It's true. There are many inappropriate prescriptions of antibiotics. Antibiotics are useful to prevent serious infections and stop bad infections from getting fatal. But even when they are used for targeting bacterial infections, there are negative effects. The main reason is the medical knowledge these days could not distinguish which bacteria has caused the infection; without an accurate diagnosis, doctors have to use a broad-spectrum antibiotic which damages lots of good bacteria and harms patient's immune system and overall health.

Rita: And bacteria will upgrade with antibiotics.

Frank: Yes, antibiotic-resistant superbugs are spreading. Like MRSA, temporarily no medicine could defeat it. But in your brother's case, using antibiotics probably do him more harm than good.

(reference: When should you take antibiotics. by Matthew Cooper)

話題二十九 Shadowing

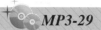 *MP3-29*

Mark: Any one has done the homework I left on last lesson? Search for how many trees we have globally.

Annie: I goggled the question and one answer is there are more than three trillion trees worldwide. A scientist used satellite data to produce a complete global map of trees and get this number.

Mark: Well done! Three trillion is an estimation of the amount. Obviously, it is impossible to count the exact number of trees on earth. Scientists have published the estimated total number as well as density of world forestry; among all the trees, about half of them are tropical/subtropical forest, one quarter grows in temperate regions and another quarter in boreal regions.

Annie: But what's the purpose of knowing how many trees we have on the planet?

Mark: Good question, it's very important. Global forestry is an abstract concept, but the number makes a specific sense. Not only the total number, scientists also found out a shocking figure: more than fifteen billion trees are lost annually. This rate is alarming; actually the world has lost almost half of its vegetational cover since the beginning of human civilization. Knowing the specific number helps people to develop targets to conserve forests. But there is also a trend that could not be caught by numbers, small trees are rapidly replacing large trees, but they are much more vulnerable to environmental change and human intervention.

Annie: I'm curious about what had people done to make the total forest halved?

Mark: It's a combination of multiple factors, such as deforestation, forest fire, drought, natural disasters, change of land use, etc. Especially in the past 50 years, we've lost trees at an unprecedented rate. Forest stocks greenhouse gas and preserves biodiversity, to maintain the forest is also protecting ourselves.

Annie: It's a shame that we did not treat the nature nicely; human beings should co-exist with other lives in harmonious.

(reference: Global count shows tree numbers have halved since dawn of human civilization)

馬克：有沒有人完成了我上一節課留的作業？搜索出全世界共有多少棵樹。

安妮：我查了這個問題，有一個答案是全球樹木總共有三萬億棵。有科學家用衛星資料，製造了完整的全球樹木分布圖，得到這個數字。

馬克：非常好！三萬億是一個估計值，顯而易見的是不可能清點出地球上所有樹木的精確數字。估量總數之外，科學家也發表了全球的森林密集度。所有的樹中，有大約一半是熱帶／亞熱帶森林，四分之一生長在溫帶，另外有四分之一分佈在北寒帶。

安妮：可是知道全世界有多少棵樹對我們來說什麼意義？

馬克：好問題，這很重要。全球林業是一個抽象的概念，但數字可以給人具體的認知。不僅是樹木總量，科學家還發現一個令人震驚的數字，每年地球都失去超過一百五十億棵樹。這是一個非常驚人的速度。實際上自從人類文明開始，地球已經失去了幾乎一半的植被保護。知曉具體數字可以幫助人們制定保護森林的目標。不過還有一個趨勢無法用數字衡量，小樹正在迅速取代大樹，可是小樹更容易受到環境變化和人類活動的干擾。

安妮：我有點好奇人們做了什麼令森林減少了一半？

馬克：是由於許多因素的綜合作用，譬如伐木、森林火災、乾旱、自然災害、土地用途變更等。尤其是在過去的五十年裡，我們失去植被的速度是空前的。森林貯藏溫室氣體，保護物種多樣化，保護森林也是保護我們自己。

安妮：真遺憾我們沒有善待自然，人類應當和其他生命和諧共生。

Recall

Mark: Any one has done the homework I left on last lesson? Search for how many trees we have globally.

Annie: I goggled the question and one answer is there are more than three trillion trees worldwide. A scientist used satellite data to produce a complete global map of trees and get this number.

Mark: Well done! Three trillion is an estimation of the amount. Obviously, it is impossible to count the exact number of trees on earth. Scientists have published the estimated total number as well as density of world forestry; among all the trees, about half of them are tropical/subtropical forest, one quarter grows in temperate regions and another quarter in boreal regions.

Annie: But what's the purpose of knowing how many trees we have on the planet?

Mark: Good question, it's very important. Global forestry is an abstract concept, but the number makes a specific sense. Not only the total number, scientists also found out a shocking figure: more than fifteen billion trees are lost annually. This rate is alarming; actually the world has lost almost half of its vegetational cover since the beginning of human civilization. Knowing the specific number helps people to develop targets to conserve forests. But there is also a trend that could not be caught by numbers. Small trees are rapidly replacing large trees, but they are much more vulnerable to environmental change and human intervention.

Annie: I'm curious about what had people done to make the total forest halved?

Mark: It's a combination of multiple factors, such as deforestation, forest fire, drought, natural disasters, change of land use, etc. Especially in the past 50 years, we've lost trees at an unprecedented rate. Forest stocks greenhouse gas and preserves biodiversity, to maintain the forest is also protecting ourselves.

Annie: It's a shame that we did not treat the nature nicely; human beings should co-exist with other lives in harmonious.

(reference: Global count shows tree numbers have halved since dawn of human civilization)

C-E

馬克：有沒有人完成了我上一節課留的作業？搜索出全世界共有多少棵樹。

安妮：我查了這個問題，有一個答案是全球樹木總共有三萬億棵。有科學家用衛星資料，製造了完整的全球樹木分布圖，得到這個數字。

馬克：非常好！三萬億是一個估計值，顯而易見的是不可能清點出地球上所有樹木的精確數字。估量總數之外，科學家也發表了全球的森林密集度。所有的樹中，有大約一半是熱帶／亞熱帶森林，四分之一生長在溫帶，另外有四分之一分佈在北寒帶。

安妮：可是知道全世界有多少棵樹對我們來說什麼意義？

馬克：好問題，這很重要。全球林業是一個抽象的概念，但數字可以給人具體的認知。不僅是樹木總量，科學家還發現一個令人震驚的數字，每年地球都失去超過一百五十億棵樹。這是一個非常驚人的速度。實際上自從人類文明開始，地球已經失去了幾乎一半的植被保護。知曉具體數字可以幫助人們制定保護森林的目標。不過還有一個趨勢無法用數字衡量，小樹正在迅速取代大樹，可是小樹更容易受到環境變化和人類活動的干擾。

安妮：我有點好奇人們做了什麼令森林減少了一半？

馬克：是由於許多因素的綜合作用，譬如伐木、森林火災、乾旱、自然災害、土地用途變更等。尤其是在過去的五十年裡，我們失去植被的速度是空前的。森林貯藏溫室氣體，保護物種多樣化，保護森林也是保護我們自己。

安妮：真遺憾我們沒有善待自然，人類應當和其他生命和諧共生。

E-C

Mark: Any one has done the homework I left on last lesson? Search for how many trees we have globally.

Annie: I goggled the question and one answer is there are more than three trillion trees worldwide. A scientist used satellite data to produce a complete global map of trees and get this number.

Mark: Well done! Three trillion is an estimation of the amount. Obviously it is impossible to count the exact number of trees on earth. Scientists has published the estimated total number as well as density of world forestry; among all the trees, about half of them are tropical/subtropical forest, one quarter grows in temperate regions and another quarter in boreal regions.

Annie: But what's the purpose of knowing how many trees we have on the planet?

Mark: Good question, it's very important. Global forestry is an abstract concept, but the number make a specific sense. Not only the total number, scientists also found out a shocking figure: more than fifteen billion trees are lost annually. This rate is alarming; actually the world has lost almost half of its vegetational cover since the beginning of human civilization. Knowing the specific number helps people to develop targets to conserve forests. But there is also a trend that could not be caught by numbers, small trees are rapidly replacing large trees, but they are much more vulnerable to environmental change and human intervention.

Annie: I'm curious about what had people done to make the total forest halved?

Mark: It's a combination of multiple factors such as deforestation, forest fire, drought, natural disasters, change of land use, etc. Especially in the past 50 years, we've lost trees at an unprecedented rate. Forest stocks greenhouse gas and preserves biodiversity, to maintain the forest is also protecting ourselves.

Annie: It's a shame that we did not treat the nature nicely; human beings should co-exist with other lives in harmonious.

(reference: Global count shows tree numbers have halved since dawn of human civilization)

Part 4
模擬試題

Part 4
模擬試題

SECTION 1 Question 1-10

Question 1-10

Complete the form below.

Write **ONE WORD AND/OR A NUMBER** for each answer.

Sigatoka Beach Resort
Example:
The customer is from **Room 606**
Dinner options
Ivy Restaurant: 　Serves seafood, especially 1_____ 　Serves root vegetables, tropical fruits 　Not recommended for 2_____
Serene Restaurant: 　Provides 3_____style food

276

Umlaut Canteen:

Saturday night theme: the 4_____dinner

Singing and dancing performed during dinner time

Sundowner Bar:

Located by the sea

Recommend burger and 5_____

Events and activities:

Activities In the Resort:

Daily activities are mostly 6_____for resort customers

The indigenous show will perform making 7_____with traditional method

Free activities: kayak adventure, ball throwing, rope pulling, 8_____class, and physical training

Need to book for Spa, scuba diving, and traditional 9_____making

Day Tours:

Sigatoka River Safari: visit local tribes and have a river trip by 10

_____

See national treasures in the Capital City

National park bush walk

Question 11-15

Choose the correct letter, **A, B** *or* **C.**

The Sydney Opera House

⑪ The Sydney Opera House is an art center of
  A visual arts
  B performing arts
  C plastic arts

⑫ What is the special feature of the vaulted ceilings in the Sydney Opera House?
  A It's more spacious than normal roof.
  B It's the world biggest one which utilises no pillars.
  C It has a semicircular shape.

⑬ Which arts company is not located in the Sydney Opera House?
  A the Australian Ballet
  B the Sydney Symphony Orchestra
  C the Musical Viva Australia

⑭ The roof 'shells' of the Sydney Opera House is composed by:
  A concrete
  B polyester
  C stone slab

⑮ The concert hall is located in which side of the Opera House?

A east

B west

C south

Question 16-20

Answer the questions below.

Write **NO MORE THAN THREE WORDS AND/OR A NUMBER** for each answer.

⑯ In which year did the completion of designing the Sydney Opera House happen?

⑰ What fruit has inspired the architect to create this special design of the building?_____

⑱ Which device did the designer team use for structure analysis during the construction?_____

⑲ Who took over the job after the original architect resigned?

_____

⑳ What has the Sydney Opera House been registered as by the UNESCO?_____

Question 21-25

Complete the sentences below.

Write **ONE WORD ONLY** for each answer.

㉑ 'Use the Library Wisely' tutorial is going to introduce the library resources and library searching_____.

㉒ The total number of all collections in the library is more than 1_____.

㉓ The Kelvin Groove branch collects materials mainly in_____ science.

㉔ The_____will provide their helps to students if they come across any difficult in the library.

㉕ The computers labs,_____rooms and group study rooms are located on level five.

Question 26-30

What action is needed when searching the library catalogue and database?

Choose **FIVE** answers from the box and write the correct letter, **A-G**, next to question 26-30.

Action

A highlight the article title

B switch the catalogue to database

C use the subject menu

D tick the item types boxes

E select the advanced search option to refine the search

F click the 'cite' tool

G select catalogue search option and type in key words

㉖ to find a book

㉗ when the result page has listed out too many results

㉘ if you are looking for results from a particular aspect_____

㉙ to search for journal articles_____

㉚ to edit the bibliography_____

Question 31-34

Complete the sentences below.

Write **NO MORE THAN TWO WORDS** for each answer.

③ All whales in the world are either baleen whales or_____ whales.

② Viviparous animals will live longer but have less_____ .

③ Whales shut their blowholes when they_____ .

④ Whales produce_____ sounds that can be heard in distance.

Question 35-40

Complete the notes below.

Write **NO MORE THAN TWO WORDS** for each answer.

Four Types of Baleen Whales

Name	Particular Character
Blue Whale	Largest animal on planet, larger than 35_____ Eat 36_____ only Was massively hunted and became an endangered species
Fin Whale	Speed of swim: 37_____ /hr Live together with other fin whales and more 38_____ than blue whales Feed on crustaceans and fishes

Grey Whale	Move to Bering Sea to feed in summer
	39 _____ trips are often arranged during winter time when they show up along the US Coast
	Has yellow and white patches on skin caused by parasites
Humpback Whale	Famous for its 40 _____
	Use special skills to catch fishes

Memo

SECTION 1 Question 1-10

Question 1-10

Complete the form below.

Write **ONE WORD AND/OR A NUMBER** for each answer.

University Accommodation Center
Example:
Looking for accommodation as an **exchange** student
Personal Information
Name: Steffi Wu
DOB: 1_____April, 1995
Major: 2_____engineering

Homestay

Ideal for start living in a new culture

The household setting is 3_____and relaxed

Average weekly price is 4_____ dollars

Some host families are very close with university

Will choose a/an 5_____host family for catering reason

University Student Apartment

The student apartment is neighbour to the 6_____

Shared bedrooms apartment share the 7_____, bathroom and living room

Single room price $399 per week, five-room share for $229

Unnecessary to 8_____internet data plan because university Wi-Fi is easy to access

Suitable for young people for its 9_____lifestyle

Gym, swimming pool and BBQ area provided

Close with convenient shops and 10_____

SECTION 2　Question 11-20

Question 11-13

Label the diagram below.

Choose THREE answers from the box and write the correct letter, **A-E**, next to questions 11-13

A Stationery Shop

B Sandwich Bar

C Blue Lotus Cafeteria

D Vietnamese Fast Food Store

E Convenient Store

The Ground Level of 44 Musk Avenue

Turkish Kebab Shop	11	12	Suncorp Bank	ATMs	The Main Gate	13	Dental Surgery	Pathology & Pharmacy

Question 14-20

*Choose the correct letter, **A, B** or **C**.*

⑭ Which service the university optometry clinics does **NOT** provide?

    A eye check for the general public

    B community education

    C merchandise of glasses

⑮ The major roles for the university clinics are educational function and providing:

    A patient care to local community

    B specialised surgical services

    C preventive treatments

⑯ The podiatry students treat patient under the supervision of:

A experienced orthopaedic surgeons

B registered podiatrists

C skilled medical doctors

⑰ The wound clinics does **NOT** care for:

A diabetic feet

B chronic vascular ulcers

C emergency wound

⑱ Which facility is located opposite to the Health Clinics on this level?

A the gym

B the swimming pool

C the Australian Red Cross

⑲ The Clinics are financially supported by:

A the federal government

B the municipal charities

C the state government

⑳ The lecture theatre on level two is also used for:

A entertainment

B religious purpose

C career fair

Question 21-25

Complete the sentences below.

Write **NO MORE THAN TWO WORDS** for each answer.

㉑ The topic of the assignment is about_____and human health.

㉒ The previous assignment is a_____which has a straight forward instruction to follow.

㉓ The most important thing to write a good assignment is to _____ early.

㉔ A good preparation will leave enough time for writing, drafting, _____and proofreading.

㉕ The_____ is a good indicator to make sure the writing is according to the assignment requirements.

Question 26-30

*Choose the correct letter, **A, B** or **C.***

㉖ One should select a smaller topic to:
   A articulate everything
   B reach specific details
   C keep within the word limit

㉗ One's opinions should be supported by:
   A evidence
   B examples
   C analysis

㉘ You figure out what specific aspects to write about after:
  A group discussion
  B brainstorming
  C reading articles

㉙ What consequence caused by forest fire could become a risk factor?
  A air pollution
  B forest degradation
  C loss of animal habitats

㉚ What is useful when creating the structure of the assignment?
  A visual map
  B time table
  C PowerPoint

SECTION 4 Question 31-40

Question 31-40

Complete the notes below.

Write **NO MORE THAN TWO WORDS** for each answer.

Koala and car accidents

Risks to Koala from human:

  Urbanization, habitat loss and segmentation

  Vehicle strikes

  31_____Attacks

  Increased prevalence of disease

Koalas are distinguished by their looks and locations

A Koala lives near human may have a name as it is considered as a

32_____ for local people

Car accidents rank second for Koala's unnatural death

A Koala hit by car may die at the scene or terribly injured

The mortality rate of Koalas sent to the emergency after being hit by car is

33_____

A baby Koala accompanied his mother during surgery has raised public

awareness

The mother Koala was hit by car and suffered facial trauma and a 34

_____

Government provide facilities to assist Koala's move

In Queensland, 35_____was built over a road where Koalas may cross

Individuals can do to limit the harm by:

   Keep with the speed limit

   Watch for Koala-crossing signs

   Slow down if find out crossing

   36_____injuries or deaths

   Wildlife friendly driving has remarkable 37_____ effect

Koalas can sleep 20 hours a day

They show up more during night from July to 38_____

Drivers find out animals from their eye shine during night drive

Animals' action can be unpredictable since the front light of the car makes the animal 39_____

Drives can carry an old blanket in the car in case they need to wrap an injured Koala

One's own safety must be protected before any intervention, 40_____ should be on while the car is safely parked

Practise Exercise 1

SECTION 1 Question 1-10

1. fish
2. children
3. western
4. Indian
5. pizza
6. free
7. fire
8. yoga
9. desert
10. motorboat

SECTION 2 Question 11-20

11. B
12. B
13. C
14. A
15. B
16. 1957
17. orange
18. computer
19. Australian architects team
20. (the) World Heritage

SECTION 3 Question 21-30

21. skills/strategies
22. million
23. social
24. librarians
25. individual
26. G
27. E
28. C
29. B
30. F

SECTION 3 Question 31-40

31. toothed
32. offspring
33. dive
34. low frequency
35. dinosaur (s)
36. krill (s)
37. 30 km
38. sociable
39. whale watching
40. songs

Practise Exercise 2

SECTION 1 Question 1-10

❶ 27th
❷ software
❸ friendly
❹ 230
❺ vegetarian
❻ campus
❼ kitchen
❽ upgrade
❾ independent
❿ restaurants

SECTION 3 Question 21-30

㉑ climate change
㉒ literature review
㉓ plan
㉔ editing
㉕ marking criteria
㉖ B
㉗ A
㉘ C
㉙ A
㉚ A

SECTION 2 Question 11-20

⑪ D
⑫ C
⑬ E
⑭ B
⑮ A
⑯ B
⑰ C
⑱ C
⑲ C
⑳ B

SECTION 4 Question 31-40

㉛ dog/domestic dog
㉜ pet
㉝ 85%/85 percent
㉞ collapsed lung/lung collapsion
㉟ overpass/over-bridge/koala-crossing infrastructure
㊱ report
㊲ protective
㊳ September
㊴ (temporarily) blind
㊵ hazard light

SECTION 1

W: Good morning! Sigatoka Beach Resort reception. How can I help you?

M: Hello. I'm the customer in <u>room 606</u>, I'd like to book a dinner for tonight in the resort. Are there any recommendations?

W: Well. We have the Ivy Restaurant that provides the Pacific Continental cuisine. It's tropical island style··· Any interests? If yes I can book you in for tonight because this one is pretty popular.

M: Sounds good. What particular we could order in this Restaurant then? I haven't really tried this kind of dishes before.

W: <u>It's mainly seafood. Fish in particular</u>, served raw or grilled. And combined with toasted root vegetables like taro and yams. The sides are tropical fruits such as pineapples, mangos and papayas. Our coconut milk is quite famous as well.

M: Ha, thank you for a nice tutorial of tropical food! Maybe we should have a try in the Ivy Restaurant.

W: Ok, let's make a reservation. Oh, because the beverage we offered there is slightly alcoholic. <u>We do not recommend this restaurant if you take children with you.</u>

M: Hmm···we do have a little girl with us. Then should I please know about any other options?

W: Of course! If you are after a formal dining, The Serene Restaurant provides memorable fine dinning. It's <u>western styled food</u>. Otherwise, the Umlaut Canteen is a nice one for children. They make themed dinners with live entertainment. Tonight is <u>Indian Saturday Night</u>. You can enjoy the Indian food, an Indian singing and dancing is performed during the dinnertime. Another option is the Sundowner Bar, which is nice and quiet. The bar is by the ocean, so you could dinning while watching the beautiful sunset scenery on the sea. This one features light dinner and we do recommend the <u>Grand Angus Beef Burger which is really kids' favorite and the wood-fired gourmet pizza is also ranked the region's best.</u>

M: Quite a lot of nice choices! I think this time I will book for the Sundowner Bar by the beach. My daughter loves pizza. She might be happy for this one. May I book for 6:30pm tonight for three people, including one child?

W: Sure! Just to confirm your room number. Is it Room 606?

M: That's correct.

W: Ok, I have booked for three persons in the Sundowner Bar tonight at six thirty. Please just mention your room number when you arrive the counter. The Bar is located in the southeast corner of the resort and you can check the map for its location. Our shuttle bus runs every 10 minutes can take you there otherwise you may walk through the Bulla Corridor. And for your information, we do have several other bistros and cafes that you don't need to book in advance.

M: Thank you very much for your help. I was also wondering is there any events and activities we could join? I'm interested in joining some day tour provided by the resort as well.

W: Yes, as you may have seen on the brochure in your room, we offer various activities. <u>Most of them are operated on a daily basis and free for our customers.</u> You can just drop-in. Like tonight at 8:30, there will be a half-hour indigenous show in the courtyard, the indigenous artists will perform the aboriginal music and they will make a fire in the traditional way.

M: Sounds very interesting! We shall go there after dinner.

W: Also every morning at 10 there will be a kayak adventure in the coast. Same time on the beach we provide ball throwing and rope pulling competition, gift is offered to the winner. If you prefer to stay in the resort, we also have free yoga class and physical training sessions; you can check the timetable for details.

M: Do I need to book for those activities?

W: No, those ones are drop-in services as well. But some items you do need to book, such as the Butterfly Spa, and that is a paid service. Lessons of scuba diving and traditional desert making are part of the accommodation package. You need to make a reservation as well.

M: Thank you! How about day tours then?

W: We are cooperating with the local travel agency to offer several tours. The most popular one is the Sigatoka river safari; you will visit several local tribes in village while on the way you can experience a river trip on motorboat. Day tour to the capital city is also recommended, several national treasures you will see over there. We also arrange the bush walk in the national park and a fishing trips to the lake near the resort. There is no extra charge for the latter two. You can refer to the visitor booklet for more trip options and details.

M: Thanks a lot! That's very informative. I will bear that in mind and make the booking soon.

W: You are very welcome! Have a good night!

M: You too!

SECTION 2

Hello everyone, I'm delighted to welcome you to the Sydney Opera House, one of the most iconic buildings in the world. Before we step inside this iconic landmark to actually discover this remarkable architecture, I will just make a brief introduction of the Opera House.

The Sydney Opera House is a performing arts center and it is obvious this is a landmark building in the city of Sydney and even a culture symbol of Australia. Every year, there are more than 1600 concerts, operas, dramas and ballets taking place here. You will later hands on the world-famous shell tiles and take a seat in the chairs of the concert hall. You may feel astonished while walking underneath the vaulted ceilings within the the world's biggest pillar-free chambers. The venues accommodate several performing arts companies, including Opera Australia, The Australian Ballet, the Sydney Theatre Company and the Sydney Symphony Orchestra. If we are lucky, later we can find a theatre rehearsal in some of the opera halls.

As you can see, the design of Sydney Opera House is quite modern and the Opera House looks different from every angle. The roof is composed by a couple of precast concrete 'shells'. The opera house is 183 meters long and 120 meters wide, and the whole building is supported by 588 concrete pillars. The two largest spaces are the concert hall in the west and the theatre in the east. Lots of smaller sized performance venues and facilities are also located inside. Surrounded the opera house, is the open public space, where free public performances are always on.

A noteworthy anecdote is the relationship between Sydney Opera House and its designer. The Opera House was designed by the famous Danish architect Jorn Utzon. He won the competition to design the Sydney Opera House in 1957. Looking from the Sydney Harbor, the Opera House resembles ships' sails or shells. You might wonder what inspired the architect to base this revolutionary design. He acknowledged in an interview that the idea came from the act of peeling an orange. The Opera House has altogether 14 shells, if combined them together, they would form a perfect sphere. Although the design was quite innovative, the construction of the Opera House was not smooth. The Opera House was supposed to be opened in 1963 at a cost of 7 million Australian dollars, but it finally opened in 1973 at a cost of around 104 million. This is mainly because the design was too much ahead of time and available technology; the high cost and extended construction period also raised lots of criticisms from the general public. Sydney Opera House was considered one of the most difficult engineering challenge in the world; since the extraordinary structure of the shells shows out like a puzzle for people who actually build them. The designer team used computer for structure analysis, which was one of the earliest use of computers in architecture. They calculated the force on each shell and figured out the sequence of assembling arches. They finally came out a solution and built up the roof. But in 1965, Sydney changed its government and the new government was not as supportive as the previous one towards the construction of the opera house. Utzon was even forced to resign and the construction leadership was handed over to Australian architects team. Luckily in late 1990s, the Opera House Trust was reconnected with Utzon and they reached reconciliation. You will later visit the "the Utzon Room" which was named after the designer to honor his contribution.

In 2007, the Sydney Opera House has become the World Heritage of the UNESCO. The official evaluation is "one of the indisputable masterpieces of human creativity". Now lets walk inside to start exploring this world heritage…

(Reference: Wikipedia page the Sydney Opera House and Jorn Utzon)

SECTION 3

Hi, I'm your librarian Hugh. Welcome to the 'use the library wisely' tutorial. In this session, I will first introduce you to the library and its resources then briefly talk about some strategies of library searching skills, which you might find helpful in future study and research.

Our university library is among one of the largest university libraries in the country, we have more than one million collections of books, e-books, journals, DVDs, CDs, maps, etc. Also we have access to hundreds of databases. This library in the Gardens Point campus is our main library, which has a comprehensive collection. This branch in the Kelvin Groove campus is the social science library and it collects materials related to education, health, art, literature, and other social science subjects. If the book you are looking for is not kept in the campus you are studying in, you can always make a request and receive it in one working day if it's available. Feeling difficult to find a book? <u>Our librarians are here to help you navigate.</u> Just don't hesitate to ask. In each level of the library, we have a number of scanners and printers for students to use. Also <u>above level five, there are computer labs, individual rooms and group study rooms</u>. You do need to book on-line for the rooms but the process is quite simple, just log on to the library main page and click "book a room"; then select the time and the room number.

Ok, now I am going to talk about how to search the library catalogue. <u>To find a book,</u> we simply go to the library main page, and <u>click on the catalogue search option. In the searching bar, type the book title, or the author's name, or subject keywords, then click the magnifier icon</u>, which will lead you to the results page. <u>You might think the result page has listed out too many items and distracted you from finding out the one you really after. So alternatively, on the top right of the main page, you find the advanced search icon, to select this option, you can refine your search</u>. For example, if you know the publication year or edition number or any specific detail of the book, just add the information in and that will reduce the number in the result page. You can tick the item types boxes to limit your search by type, like this, by selecting only the "e-books", we limit the searching results to show e-books only. <u>You can also refine your searching results by using the subject menu.</u> For example, if you type the key word "sustainable development", to the left you find the results are categorized into different aspects, such as economic aspect, environmental aspect, political aspect, cultural aspect, etc. You can just select the subject to view results only in your desired area, the results become smaller but precise.

Now let's have a look of how to find journal articles. In the main page, <u>you need to switch the catalogue to database</u> in the <u>searching bar that would lead you to the article databases.</u> If you already know the database name, simply type the name into the searching bar and go directly to the database. Otherwise you can chose database by subject. To search within a database, you just combine several of the key words into the search boxes. The advanced search features of each database will generally lead you to refine the searching results. Move the cursor on the title of an article; the information about it will come out in a new window. Databases also help with your citations, <u>the "cite" tool could export formatted citation to your EndNote or other citation manager, save up your time to edit the bibliography</u>. Be aware sometimes the article title would not bring you directly to the full article, you might need to try other databases to see if article is available somewhere else. This is a brief introduction to the general use of our library, any questions please…

(Reference: website of QUT library, University of Wisconsin-Madison Libraries, University of Illinois Library)

SECTION 4

Stefanie: Hi everyone, the topic our group selected for the wildlife case study is the whale. Now I will first present the general features and several species of whales then my group mates will continue with more detailed information.

There are more than 90 species of whales, all whale species can be categorised into baleen whales and toothed whales. The baleen whales eat by swimming slowly through fish-rich water and straining food into their mouth. And toothed whales as their names indicate, have teeth. Whales live in marine environment and they are mammals. Just like the continental mammals, whales are also viviparous, which means they reproduce by giving birth to a calf rather than eggs, which leads to fewer offspring and longer-lived individuals. Whales breath with their lungs, and they all have blowholes positioned on top of their head. They breathe in air through the blowholes when they are on the water surface and close it up when they dive. All mammals need to sleep, but whales have to be awake all the time to maintain breath. So whales have a special sleep pattern: half of their brain falls asleep while the other half keeps awake, that makes whales to sleep 24 hours per day. Whales have very advanced hearing and they can hear from miles away. They produce low frequency sound, which can be detected over large distances. Now many species of whales are declared as endangered. Apart from human activities such as illegal whaling, these animals could collide with ships or entangled with fishing nets. They are also threatened by pollution and habitat loss from climate change.

Now I will briefly talk about four types of baleen whales. The first one is the blue whale. The blue whale is the largest animal on the planet. It is also the largest animals ever to have lived, since they are much larger than dinosaurs. Their heart has the same size of a small car, which bumps tons of blood through the circulatory system of the blue whale. The largest blue whale that ever found was 33.58 meters long and weighs 190 tons. The skin of the blue whale is blue-grey colored. On top of its head, there is a large ridge located from the tip of the nose to the blowhole. The blue whale has a very small dorsal fin and relatively small tail flukes. In terms of feeding and distribution, the blue whale feeds almost exclusively on krill and you can find the blue whales worldwide. They travel to polar waters to feed during summer time and spend the winter in tropical or subtropical oceans. Blue whale likes to swim alone or in groups of 2 or 3. In the past century, blue whale has been extensively hunted and the number has decreased to very low level. Hence, It Is now listed as endangered species.

The second one I will introduce is the fin whale. The fin whale is a fast swimmer. It could swim at the speed of 30 km/hr. Occasionally, the fin whale would jump out of the water. The average length of the fin whale is about 18 to 22 meters and could weigh up to 70 tons. The fin whale looks long and slender, the head resembles the blue whale but the color is dark grey to brown. The fin whale prefers to stay in deep water and it is also distributed all over the world ocean. Unlike the blue whale, fin whale is more gregarious, which means they live in flocks and more sociable. Fin whales are generally seen in groups of 10 or more. They mainly feed on small crustaceans such as crabs, lobsters and shrimps. Northern hemisphere fin whales also feed on fish.

Next one is the grey whale, which appears only in the North Pacific Ocean. The grey whale is baleen whale as well. In summer the grey whale move to the Bering Sea to feed and in winter they travel along the US coast down to the Mexico coast. There are lots of whale watching trips organised and sometimes they swim very close to the whale watching boats. The size of the grey whale is relatively smaller comparing with the previous two types. They are 15 meters long on average and weigh about 20 tons. The skin of the back of the grey whale has yellow and white coloured patches caused by parasites. Grey whales is also critically endangered and granted protection from commercial hunting; therefore, they are no longer hunted on a large scale.

The forth one on our list is the humpback whale. This is probably the most famous whale species because of its songs that could be heard from far distance. Only the male sings. So there is a hypothesis that the humpback whale's song has a reproductive propose. Humpback whale is black all over, and it has a unique way of catching fish, it dives down and circles to the surface. On the way up, fishes are encircled in a bubble net and swallowed by the humpback whale. This type of whale also travels long distance; they spend winter near Hawaii and move to the polar regions in summer. The humpback whale is up to 19 meters long and 48 tons weight. It feeds on krill, sardines and small fishes. The humpback whale is considered as a vulnerable species and whaling is prohibited as well.

(Reference: marine mammals http://www.sarkanniemi.fi/akatemiat/ eng_spe1.html#)

Practise Exercise 2

SECTION 1

M: Good morning, Bond University accommodation center! How can I help you?

W: Good morning, I've just been accepted as an exchange student in the university and I will start from next semester. I'd like to arrange an accommodation from next semester until Christmas time. I found your contact detail from the university website, may I arrange a living place from you before I arrive Australia?

M: Yes, definitely! I just need to document some of your personal information as well as your preference. Then we can start to make the selection from there.

W: Ok! Thank you.

M: Now, first of all, may I have you name please?

W: It's Steffi Wu. My given name spells S-T-E-F-F-I.

M: Thanks, and your date of birth please.

W: It's 27th April 1995.

M: Ok, and may I ask your major please?

W: It's software engineering under the course name of computer science.

M: Thank you. Have you already decided which kind of accommodation you would like to choose? Like university apartment? Or homestay? Or share house?

W: Hmm, I'm considering choosing between the homestay and the university apartment. I haven't lived with a host family before, would you mind provide me some information please?

M: Of course not! Generally, homestay is ideal for starting living in a new culture; it's easy and comfortable because you stay in a relaxed and friendly household setting. The host family will provide you with all the basic needs. You will have your own room. The homestay parents will do the laundry for you. Breakfast and dinner are provided and you can talk with the host family to see if they offer lunch. You pay weekly and the average price is around 230 Australia dollars per week. All the host families that cooperate with our universities had a good record so the only thing you think about is the location.

W: Sounds very good. And I can make friends with a local family. Just wondering normally how close will I live to the university is a reasonable distance, my friend who studied in Australia last semester told me not to expect living too close to uni.

M: Ha, yes. A thirty-minute to one hour travel time is the most possible case but this will depend on the area close to the university. We do have some host family that is really close with the uni. If you are looking for a close one, I can check the vacancy for you. Apart from the location, do you have any other particular requirements?

W: Hmm, I am a vegetarian. If the host family is also vegetarian that would be great, otherwise I can cook myself.

M: Ok, here we do have a large proportion of people who are vegetarian as well. I will note this down for you and set this into our selection criteria if you later decide to choose a homestay.

W: Thank you! Before moving forward, I might also ask about the student accommodation as well.

M: Definitely. The uni dorm is really convenient since it is located right next to the campus. It offers fully furnished apartments. You can select from one bedroom to six-bedroom share. For the multiple bedroom apartments, you share the kitchen, bathroom, and the living room. The advantage of living in the student apartment is obvious because it's only ten minutes walking to your lecture.

W: This really attracts me. What about the price then?

M: Well, the studio is the most expensive; it's 399 dollars per week. Three-bedroom share is 299 and five-bedroom share is 229.

W: Is the utilities included in the price?

M: Yes, all bills included and you have 10GB of Internet data. You can upgrade the data plan if that's not enough, but I don't think you need that, the library is the next door and you can just use the university Wi-Fi.

W: That's really good!

M: And young people like you would prefer the independent lifestyle. Also there is an on-site gym, outdoor swimming pool and a BBQ area. Another merit is you get access to convenient shops and restaurants on your doorstep.

W: I think I will choose the university apartment although homestay sounds quite nice as well.

M: Ok! Please give me your email address and I will send you the application form.

SECTION 2

Now I'm going to introduce this multifunctional building the 44 Musk Avenue. This building is located inside the university complex and it is a university property, while several companies are currently utilizing it. This building has four levels and it was opened six years ago.

On Ground level are shops facing the Musk Avenue, which are

quite convenient for the residents in the Kelvin Groove Urban Village as well as the university students. The restaurant in the west corner is the Turkish Kebab shop. The next door is the Vietnamese fast food store; it sells rice paper roll and other bakeries. Then is the Blue Lotus Cafeteria, which is famous for its coffee and breakfast. Next to the cafe is a branch of the Suncorp Bank, and several ATMs from other banks as well. Then you see the main gate to the building. On the other side of the gate, there are a convenient store, a dental surgery, and a pharmacy with pathology room respectively.

Two facilities located on the ground level. When you walk in through the main gate, on the left hand side is the University Optometry clinic. It is open to the public. You can get your eyes checked in the optometry clinic and they sell good quality glasses as well. The university clinic's main roles are providing education to the allied-health students and quality patient care to the community. The services are quite reputable too. Walking further down to the end is the swimming pool, which is a part of the health-stream gym. The swimming pool is open to the gym members and quite often the local kindergarten and primary school will use it for their students.

Level one has the university health clinics and the gym as well. The podiatry and wound care clinics are also open to the public. In the podiatry clinic, all treatments are done by students and they work under instruction of experienced clinical supervisors who are also registered podiatrists. The biomechanics and gait analysis would find out the foot abnormality and functional orthotics would be made to support the patients walking. Pediatric podiatry clinics provide kids with foot care. Very experienced nursing practitioners specialized in wound care work in <u>the wound clinics, where patients with chronic wound such as diabetic foot or vascular ulcer in the lower limbs can be checked and cared on a regular basis.</u> Next to the health clinics is the gym and the gym is located right above the swimming pool. The gym upstairs offers various exercise equipment plus training courses. <u>On the opposite side of the clinics is the Australian Red Cross office</u>; it also has a blood bank inside.

Level two has the other part of the university health clinics, which is the psychology and counseling clinic. It is advertised that a new eating disorder and weight management clinic is planned to be opened later this year. It is very cost effective to use the clinics because the university is a public university and the <u>clinics are also sponsored by the state government</u>. Patients pay one-third of the normal price and get high quality service. Beside the clinic is the university medical service; several general practitioners are located in this facility. This medical center serves the university students and staff exclusively. There is a lecture theatre and several smaller sized classrooms on level two as well, they are mainly used by the students from the faculty of health. Every Friday at midday, <u>the lecture theatre is temporarily used as a prayers room for religious propose</u>.

Level three is currently vacant for rent. It was a construction company previously located there.

The 44 Musk Avenue has underground car parks, with the capacity of around 300 parking lots. The building management office and the garbage collection house are also located at the basement. In case of a fire or other emergencies, people inside of the building will be evacuated into the Mccaskie Park via the safety gate facing west side on level one.

SECTION 3

Tutor: Hi, Jacky, have you checked the blackboard? The assignment has been released.

Jacky: Thanks Lisa. Yes I have just seen it. It's quite broad, <u>we can pick up any aspect that is related with climate change and human health</u>, then discuss about it. I think it's actually harder compared with more specific topics.

Tutor: Truly it is. It's harder than the previous one.

Jacky: <u>Yes, at least the literature review has a very clear instruction to follow</u>; but this one I'm even stuck at picking up a topic.

Tutor: Don't worry. Most people feel the same way. You will gradually work through it. Just spend your time on it, the picture will become more and more clear.

Jacky: I think so too. Lisa, would you mind guiding me through the topic or maybe giving me some advice.

Tutor: Ok, do you know the word limit?

Jacky: It's no more than five thousand words.

Tutor: Alright, then you can plan the assignment according to the word count. <u>Remember the key to write a good assignment is to plan early</u>. Actually more than half of the time you spend on a writing task should be at the planning. Figure out what you want to write, do some research, read the articles and write the structure out. After sorting out all those preparations, you then move to the first draft.

Jacky: That means most effort has been done before writing.

Tutor: Yes, after good preparation, your writing will become very smooth. <u>And you still have enough time left for writing, drafting, editing and proofreading etc</u>. So start early and you will stress less.

Jacky: That's what I'm doing now. I have six weeks before the due date.

Tutor: Very good. <u>You could always refer to the marking criteria to make sure you meet the assignment requirements.</u> If you aim for distinction, you should address the assignment question very clearly, maybe also produce something creative.

Jacky: The question is "discuss the climate change and human health". It's impossible to explain that properly in five thousand words. I may focus on smaller topics like 'the heat waves and its influence to people in tropical areas'.

Tutor: You are on the right track! Be focused is essential for a good assignment. You can't articulate everything properly in such a word limit if the research area is so broad. <u>Make your topic smaller and get into details</u>. And the topic you choose is absolutely fine.

Jacky: Ok, if I will write that topic, should I start with browsing the database?

Tutor: Well we first analyse the question. its direction word is 'discuss', which means you present a subject, and give your points of view about it. You need to support your view with evidence-based information. Be aware analysis and opinions are equally important. The topic words are the 'climate change' and the 'human health', and what you have done is narrowing them down to 'heat wave' and 'people in tropical areas'. I suggest you can further narrow the people living in tropical areas down to people living in a single country such as Pakistan or Bangladesh, which will make your research easier. Now you get key words for literature search. After reading several articles, you will find out which specific aspects you would like to discuss about.

Jacky: Thank you Lisa, so I need to figure out the question clearly and start from there. Just wondering which aspect of human health I should address, that's pretty wide too.

Tutor: Yes, human health is quite a broad issue, and it's better to be clearly defined. Like what I have suggested, you've picked up people from their geographic location then focus on a single country. Within that country, you can select a certain group of people, consider factors like children under five-year-old, or people with low social-economic status, or even smokers. For that certain group of people, what are the health risks posed by heat waves? Over what temperature, people would feel uncomfortable? Would they become more vulnerable to chronic disease or epidemic disease under heat waves?

Jacky: I see.

Tutor: Think about the climate, are there any changes in the length, frequency and intensity of heat waves. Find out more risk factors associated with heat waves, such as forest fire and consequent air pollution. Lots of things to think about.

Jacky: Like brainstorming the question.

Tutor: Exactly. Heat waves is just an example. For any topic you choose, do the same thing. You can draw visual maps or tables. Jot down ideas and questions. This will help you to generate the structure. Then you start the research and reading. If stuck, ask yourself some questions. Use the W questions, ask "what, where, when, why, how, who, which", ideas will gradually come out.

Jacky: Thank you Lisa, I've got very valuable advice. Will start to work on it now.

Tutor: Good luck with the assignment.

Jacky: Thanks!

SECTION 4

Koalas are recognised as symbol of Australia, but the species face many threats in this modernised world. Land exploitation in areas where koalas used to live has posed various risks to this cute creature. Urbanization is depriving and fragmenting koala habitat; human-induced threats such as vehicle strikes or domestic dog attacks are also threatening koala's life. It is also believed the increased prevalence of koala's diseases are to some extent due to the stress caused by human activities.

Some koalas live in the sanctuary where they are cared by the experienced staff. While most koalas live in the wild they are easily recognized by their appearance and the habitat they are from. Koalas may be given a nickname by local residents if they show up frequently in the neighborhood, so they are more like human's pets rather than a wild animals. People enjoy seeing koalas and they make lots of effort to protect them, such as planting trees and controlling their dogs.

The biggest threat to koala's existence is habitat destruction, and following this, the most serious threat is death from car hits. I'm going to talk about the koala and the car accident. A koala hit by vehicle could be killed straight away or suffering serious injuries. The figure from the Australian Wildlife Hospital and another koala rescue center shows that 3792 koalas were taken to the hospitals between 1997 and 2008, and 85% of the injured koalas died after emergency procedures. This number is only the ones that have been calculated, so at least more than 300 koalas are killed each year by motor vehicles.

On June 11 2015, a 6-month-old baby koala Phantom clung to his mother during her life-saving surgery after she was hit by a car in Brisbane, Australia. The photo of Phantom with Lizzy has attracted thousands of views. The mother Lizzy suffered severe injuries including facial trauma and a collapsed lung. Phantom stayed by his mom's side throughout the entire operation. Luckily Lizzy started recovering after the surgery. How to prevent this kind of situation from happening in the first place has raised the public awareness.

The Australia government has made a good effort to protect koala form car accidents. When you drive in Queensland, sometimes you can see an overpass built on top of a road. The over-bridge is the koala-crossing infrastructure. The state government has made guidelines for koala safety and required in areas where traffic flow pose risks to koalas, facilities assisting safe koala movement should be built.

At individual level, although it may seem that there is not much we can do since the wild animals cannot be restricted from rushing out onto a road. There are still several things drivers can do to protect koalas, including obeying the speed limit, watching for koala crossing signs, slowing down if see koalas crossing, especially during the night, and report injured or dead koala if see one.

Wildlife-friendly driving would benefit koalas. The risk of hitting can be reduced by avoid driving in areas where koalas appear. Driving slowly within the speed limit and scanning the roadside for anything that may move onto the road have significant preventive effect.

Koalas can sleep up to twenty hours per day and not come to the ground very often. However, nowadays their habitat is fragmented by development. So they have to cross roads to reach some of the food trees. Koala crossing signs is a good indicator to inform drivers that have entered koala's territory. The peak time for them to move across road is most likely to be between July and September usually during the night. If driving through koala habitat during 'koala peak hour', drivers should slow down and check the roadside for koalas and other wild animals.

During the night, koalas crossing the road would have eye shining. Their eyes reflect the headlights of coming vehicles, which would alert drivers. Driving slowly will give drivers enough time to reflect and avoid the hit. Animals' action would be unpredictable since they might become temporarily blind when confronted by bright light at night, but slowing down can give them time to get off the road.

What could people do if they a koala accidentally or encounter an injured koala? It is recommended carrying an old towel or blanket in the car. So the injured koala could be wrapped and moved out off the road. Local wildlife care groups or vet surgery can be contacted. <u>Most importantly, people should always consider their own safety before intervening, cars need to be parked safely with hazard light on to alert other drivers.</u> Call the wildlife care groups if you are sure what actions to take. People who are interested in caring the sick koalas can even attend certain training programs on wildlife rehabilitation to get useful information.

英語學習 ─生活・文法・考用─

定價：NT$369元/K$116元
規格：320頁/17＊23cm/MP3

定價：NT$380元/HK$119元
規格：320頁/17＊23cm/MP3

定價：NT$349元/HK$109元
規格：352頁/17＊23cm

定價：NT$380元/HK$119元
規格：288頁/17＊23cm/MP3

定價：NT$329元/HK$103元
規格：352頁/17＊23cm

定價：NT$349元/HK$109元
規格：304頁/17＊23cm

定價：NT$380元/HK$119元
規格：352頁/17＊23cm

定價：NT$369元/HK$115元
規格：304頁/17＊23cm/MP3

定價：NT$380元/HK$119元
規格：304頁/17＊23cm/MP3

Learn Smart! 058

猴腮雷 雅思聽力 7+ (附 MP3)

作　　者	武董
發 行 人	周瑞德
執行總監	齊心瑀
企劃編輯	陳韋佑
校　　對	編輯部
封面構成	高鍾琪

內頁構成	菩薩蠻數位文化有限公司
印　　製	大亞彩色印刷製版股份有限公司
初　　版	2016 年 5 月
定　　價	新台幣 380 元
出　　版	倍斯特出版事業有限公司
電　　話	(02) 2351-2007
傳　　真	(02) 2351-0887
地　　址	100 台北市中正區福州街 1 號 10 樓之 2
E - m a i l	best.books.service@gmail.com
網　　址	www.bestbookstw.com

港澳地區總經銷	泛華發行代理有限公司
地　　址	香港新界將軍澳工業邨駿昌街 7 號 2 樓
電　　話	(852) 2798-2323
傳　　真	(852) 2796-5471

國家圖書館出版品預行編目資料

猴腮雷：雅思聽力 7+ / 武董著. --
初版. -- 臺北市：倍斯特, 2016.05
面；　公分. --(Learn smart!；58)
ISBN 978-986-92855-1-3（平裝附光碟片）
1. 國際英語語文測試系統 2. 考試指南

　805.189　　　　　　　　105005765